PENGUIN BOOKS

LOOKING FOR RACH

Robert B. Parker was born in 1932 and has a Ph.D. from Boston University. He has been Professor of English at Northeastern University, Massachusetts, U.S.A., teaching courses in American literature, and has written several serious textbooks including *The Personal Response to Literature*. He has written numerous other novels featuring his wry Boston private detective, Spenser; of these Penguin publish *The Godwulf Manuscript*, *God Save the Child*, *Mortal Stakes*, *A Promised Land*, *The Judas Goat*, *A Savage Place*, *Valediction*, *Early Autumn*, *Ceremony* and *A Catskill Eagle*. *Promised Land* won the Edgar Allan Poe Award in the U.S.A. for the best mystery novel of 1976.

Robert Parker has also written two non-Spenser novels, *Wilderness* and *Love and Glory*. An enthusiastic sportsman, he is the author of *Sports Illustrated Weights Training*. He lives in Cambridge, Massachusetts, with his wife, Joan, and his hobbies include jogging and canoeing.

Looking for Rachel Wallace

Robert B. Parker

PENGUIN BOOKS

For Joan, David and Daniel
– my good fortune

Penguin Books Ltd, Harmondsworth, Middlesex, England
Viking Penguin Inc., 40 West 23rd Street, New York, New York 10010, U.S.A.
Penguin Books Australia Ltd, Ringwood, Victoria, Australia
Penguin Books Canada Limited, 2801 John Street, Markham, Ontario, Canada L3R 1B4
Penguin Books (N.Z.) Ltd, 182–190 Wairau Road, Auckland 10, New Zealand

First published in the U.S.A. by Delacorte Press/Seymour Lawrence 1980
Published in Great Britain by Penguin Books 1987

Made and printed in Great Britain by
Richard Clay Ltd, Bungay, Suffolk

1

LOCKE-OBER'S RESTAURANT is on Winter Place, which is an alley off Winter Street just down from the Common. It is Old Boston the way the Custom House tower is Old Boston. The decor is plain. The waiters wear tuxedos. There are private dining rooms. Downstairs is a room which used to be the Men's Bar until it was liberated one lunchtime by a group of humorless women who got into a shouting match with a priest. Now anybody can go in there and do what they want. They take Master Charge.

I didn't need Master Charge. I wasn't paying, John Ticknor was paying. And he didn't need Master Charge, because he was paying with the company's money. I ordered lobster Savannah. The company was Hamilton Black Publishing, and they had ten million dollars. Ticknor ordered scrod.

"And two more drinks, please."

"Very good." The waiter took our menus and hurried off. He had a hearing aid in each ear.

Ticknor finished his Negroni. "You drink only beer, Mr. Spenser?"

The waiter returned with a draft Heineken for me and another Negroni for Ticknor.

"No. I'll drink wine sometimes."

"But no hard liquor?"

"Not often. I don't like it. I like beer."

"And you always do what you like."

"Almost always. Sometimes I can't."

He sipped some more Negroni. Sipping didn't look easy for him.

"What might prevent you?" he said.

"I might have to do something I don't like in order to get to do something I like a lot."

Ticknor smiled a little. "Metaphysical," he said.

I waited. I knew he was trying to size me up. That was okay, I was used to that. People didn't know anything about hiring someone like me, and they almost always vamped around for a while.

"I like milk, too," I said. "Sometimes I drink that."

Ticknor nodded. "Do you carry a gun?" he said.

"Yes."

The waiter brought our salad.

"How tall are you?"

"Six one and something."

"How much do you weigh?"

"Two-oh-one and a half, this morning, after running."

"How far do you run?"

The salad was made with Boston lettuce and was quite fresh.

"I do about five miles a day," I said. "Every once in a while I'll do ten to sort of stretch out."

"How did your nose get broken?"

"I fought Joe Walcott once when he was past his prime."

"And he broke your nose?"

"If he'd been in his prime, he'd have killed me," I said.

"You were a fighter then."

I nodded. Ticknor was washing down a bite of salad with the rest of his Negroni.

"And you've been on the police?"

I nodded.

"And you were dismissed?"

"Yeah."

"Why?"

"They said I was intractable."

"Were they right?"

"Yeah."

The waiter brought our entrée.

"I am told that you are quite tough."

"You betcha," I said. "I was debating here today whether to have lobster Savannah or just eat one of the chairs."

Ticknor smiled again, but not like he wanted me to marry his sister.

"I was also told that you were—I believe the phrase was, and I'm quoting—'a smart-mouthed bastard'—though it was not said without affection."

I said, "Whew."

Ticknor ate a couple of green peas from the side dish. He was maybe fifty and athletic-looking. Squash probably, tennis. Maybe he rode. He wore rimless glasses, which you don't see all that often anymore, and had a square-jawed Harvardy face, and an unkempt gray crew cut like Archibald Cox. Not a patsy even with the Bryn Mawr accent. Not soft.

"Were you thinking of commissioning a biography of me, or do you want to hire me to break someone's arm?"

"I know some book reviewers," he said, "but . . . no, neither of those." He ate five more peas. "Do you know very much about Rachel Wallace?"

"*Sisterhood*," I said.

"Really?"

"Yeah. I have an intellectual friend. Sometimes she reads to me."

"What did you think of it?"

"I thought Simone de Beauvoir already said most of it."

"Have you read *The Second Sex*?"

"Don't tell the guys down the gym," I said. "They'll think I'm a fairy."

"We published *Sisterhood*."

"Oh, yeah?"

"Nobody ever notices the publisher. But yes, we did. And we're publishing her new book."

"What is that called?"

"*Tyranny*."

"Catchy title."

"It is an unusual book," Ticknor said. "The tyrants are people in high places who discriminate against gay women."

"Catchy idea," I said.

Ticknor frowned for a moment. "The people in high places are named. Ms. Wallace has already had threats against her if the book is published."

"Ah-hah," I said.

"I beg your pardon?"

"My role in this is beginning to take on definition."

"Oh, yes, the threats. Well, yes. That's it essentially. We want you to protect her."

"Two hundred dollars a day," I said. "And expenses."

"Expenses?"

"Yeah, you know. Sometimes I run out of ammunition and have to buy more. Expenses."

"There are people I can get for half that."

"Yeah."

The waiter cleared the lunch dishes and poured coffee.

"I'm not authorized to go that high."

I sipped my coffee.

"I can offer one hundred thirty-five dollars a day."

I shook my head.

Ticknor laughed. "Have you ever been a literary agent?" he said.

"I told you, I don't do things I don't like to do if I can avoid it."

"And you don't like to work for a hundred and thirty-five a day."

I nodded.

"Can you protect her?"

"Sure. But you know as well as I do that it depends on what I protect her from. I can't prevent a psychopath from sacrificing himself to kill her. I can't prevent a horde of hate-crazed sexists from descending on her. I can make her harder to hurt, I can up the cost to the hurter. But if she wishes to live anything like a normal life, I can't make her completely safe."

"I understand that," Ticknor said. He didn't look happy about it, though.

"What about the cops?" I said.

"Ms. Wallace doesn't trust them. She sees them as, quote, 'agents of repression.' "

"Oh."

"She has also said she refuses to have, and once again I quote, 'a rabble of armed thugs following me about day and night.' She has agreed to a single bodyguard. At first she insisted on a woman."

"But?"

"But if there were to be but one, we felt a man might be better. I mean if you had to wrestle with an assassin, or whatever. A man would be stronger, we felt."

"And she agreed?"

"Without enthusiasm."

"She gay?" I said.

"Yes," Ticknor said.

"And out of the closet?"

"Aggressively out of the closet," Ticknor said. "Does that bother you?"

"Gay, no. Aggressive, yes. We're going to spend a lot of time together. I don't want to fight with her all day."

"I can't say it will be pleasant, Spenser. She's not an easy person. She has a splendid mind, and she has forced the world to listen to her. It has been difficult. She's tough and cynical and sensitive to every slight."

"Well, I'll soften her up," I said. "I'll bring some candy and flowers, sweet-talk her a little . . ."

Ticknor looked like he'd swallowed a bottle cap.

"My God, man, don't joke with her. She'll simply explode."

Ticknor poured some more coffee for me and for himself from the small silver pot. There was only one other table occupied now. It made no difference to our waiter. He sprang forward when Ticknor put the coffeepot down, took it away, and returned almost at once with a fresh pot.

"The only reservation I have," Ticknor said when the waiter had retreated, "is the potential for a personality clash."

I leaned back in my chair and folded my arms.

"You look good in most ways," Ticknor said. "You've got the build for it. People who should know say you are as tough as you look. And they say you're honest. But you work awfully hard sometimes at being a wise guy. And you look like everything Rachel hates."

"It's not hard work," I said.

"What isn't?"

"Being a wise guy. It's a gift."

"Perhaps," Ticknor said. "But it is not a gift that will endear you to Rachel Wallace. Neither will the muscles and the machismo."

"I know a guy would lend me a lavender suit," I said.

"Don't you want this work?" Ticknor said.

I shook my head. "What you want, Mr. Ticknor, is someone feisty enough to get in the line of someone else's fire, and tough enough to get away with it. And you want him to look like Winnie-the-Pooh and act like Rebecca of Sunnybrook Farm. I'm not sure Rebecca's even got a gun permit."

He was silent for a moment. The other table cleared, and now we were alone in the upstairs dining room, except for several waiters and the maître d'.

"God damn it," Ticknor said. "You are right. If you'll take the job, it's yours. Two hundred dollars a day and expenses. And God help me, I hope I'm right."

"Okay," I said. "When do I meet Ms. Wallace?"

2

I MET RACHEL WALLACE on a bright October day when Ticknor and I walked down from his office across the Common and the Public Garden through the early turn-of-fall foliage and visited her in her room at the Ritz.

She didn't look like Carry Nation. She looked like a pleasant woman about my age with a Diane Von Furstenberg dress on and some lipstick, and her hair long and black and clean.

Ticknor introduced us. She shook hands firmly and looked at me carefully. If I'd had tires, she'd have kicked them. "Well, you're better than I expected," she said.

"What did you expect?" I said.

"A wide-assed ex-policeman with bad breath wearing an Anderson Little suit."

"Everybody makes mistakes," I said.

"Let's have as few as possible between us," she said. "To

insure that, I think we need to talk. But not here. I hate hotel rooms. We'll go down to the bar."

I said okay. Ticknor nodded. And the three of us went down to the bar. The Ritz is all a bar should be—dark and quiet and leathery, with a huge window that looks out onto Arlington Street and across it to the Public Garden. The window is tinted so that the bar remains dim. I always like to drink in the Ritz Bar. Ticknor and Rachel Wallace had martinis on the rocks. I had beer.

"That figures," Rachel Wallace said, when I ordered the beer.

"Everybody laughs at me when I order a Pink Lady," I said.

"John has warned me that you are a jokester. Well, I am not. If we are to have any kind of successful association, you'd best understand right now that I do not enjoy humor. Whether or not successful."

"Okay if now and then I enjoy a wry, inward smile if struck by one of life's vagaries?"

She turned to Ticknor, and said, "John, he won't do. Get rid of him."

Ticknor took a big drink of his martini. "Rachel, damn it. He's the best around at what we need. You did needle him about the beer. Be reasonable, Rachel."

I sipped some beer. There were peanuts in a small bowl in the center of the table. I ate some.

"He's read your book," Ticknor said. "He'd read it even before I approached him."

She took the olive on a toothpick out of her drink and bit half of it off and held the other half against her bottom lip and looked at me. "What did you think of *Sisterhood*?"

"I think you are rehashing Simone de Beauvoir."

Her skin was quite pale and the lipstick mouth was very bright against it. It made her smile more noticeable. "Maybe you'll do," she said. "I prefer to think that I'm reapplying Simone de Beauvoir to contemporary issues. But I'll accept 'rehashing.' It's direct. You speak your mind."

I ate some more peanuts.

"Why did you read Simone de Beauvoir?"

"My friend gave it to me for my birthday. She recommended it."

"What did you feel was her most persuasive insight?"

"Her suggestion that women occupied the position of *other*. Are we having a quiz later?"

"I wish to get some insight into your attitude toward women and women's issues."

"That's dumb," I said. "You ought to be getting insight into how well I can shoot and how hard I can hit and how quick I can dodge. That's what somebody is giving me two hundred a day for. My attitude toward women is irrelevant. So are my insights into *The Second Sex*."

She looked at me some more. She leaned back against the black leather cushions of the corner banquette where we sat. She rubbed her hands very softly together.

"All right," she said. "We shall try. But there are ground rules. You are a big attractive man. You have probably been successful in your dealings with some women. I am not like those women. I am a lesbian. I have no sexual interest in you or any other man. Therefore there is no need for flirtatious behavior. And no need to take it personally. Does the idea of a gay woman offend you or titillate you?"

"Neither of the above," I said. "Is there a third choice?"

"I hope so," she said. She motioned to the waiter and ordered another round. "I have work to do," she went on. "I have books to write and publicize. I have speeches to give and causes to promote and a life to live. I will not stay in some safe house and hide while my life goes by. I will not change what I am, whatever the bigots say and do. If you want to do this, you'll have to understand that."

"I understand that," I said.

"I also have an active sex life. Not only active but often diverse. You'll have to be prepared for that, and you'll have to conceal whatever hostility you may feel toward me or the women I sleep with."

"Do I get fired if I blush?"

"I told you before, I have no sense of humor. Do you agree or disagree?"

"Agree."

"Finally, except when you feel my life is in danger, I want you to stay out of my way. I realize you will have to be around and watchful. I don't know how serious the threats are, but you have to assume they are serious. I understand that. But short of a mortal situation I do not want to hear from you. I want a shadow."

I said, "Agree," and drank the rest of my beer. The waiter came by and removed the empty peanut bowl and replaced it. Rachel Wallace noticed my beer was gone and gestured that the waiter should bring another. Ticknor looked at his glass and at Rachel Wallace's. His was empty, hers wasn't. He didn't order.

"Your appearance is good," she said. "That's a nice suit, and it's well tailored. Are you dressed up for the occasion or do you always look good?"

"I'm dressed up for the occasion. Normally I wear a light-blue body stocking with a big red **S** on the front." It was dim in the bar, but her lipstick was bright, and I thought for a moment she smiled, or nearly smiled, or one corner of her mouth itched.

"I want you presentable," she said.

"I'll be presentable, but if you want me appropriate, you'll have to let me know your plans ahead of time."

She said, "Certainly."

I said thank you. I tried to think of things other than the peanuts. One bowl was enough.

"I've had my say, now it is your turn. You must have some rules or questions, or whatever. Speak your mind."

I drank beer. "As I said to Mr. Ticknor when he and I first talked, I cannot guarantee your safety. What I can do is increase the odds against an assassin. But someone dedicated or crazy can get you."

"I understand that," she said.

"I don't care about your sex life. I don't care if you elope with Anita Bryant. But I do need to be around when it happens. If you make it with strangers, you might be inviting your murderer to bed."

"Are you suggesting I'm promiscuous?"

"You suggested it a little while ago. If you're not, it's not a problem. I don't assume your friends will kill you."

"I think we'll not discuss my sex life further. John, for God's sake order another drink. You look so uncomfortable, I'm afraid you'll discorporate."

He smiled and signaled the waiter.

"Do you have any other statements to make?" she said to me.

"Maybe one more," I said. "I hire on to guard your body, that's what I'll do. I will work at it. Part of working at it will include telling you things you can do and things you can't do. I know my way around this kind of work a lot better than you do. Keep that in mind before you tell me to stick it. I'll stay out of your way when I can, but I can't always."

She put her hand out across the table, and I took it. "We'll try it, Spenser," she said. "Maybe it won't work, but it could. We'll try."

3

"OKAY," I SAID, "tell me about the death threats."

"I've always gotten hate mail. But recently I have gotten some phonecalls."

"How recently?"

"As soon as the bound galleys went out."

"What are bound galleys? And who do they go out to?"

Ticknor spoke. "Once a manuscript is set in type, a few copies are run off to be proofread by both author and copy editor. These are called galley proofs."

"I know that part," I said. "What about the bound ones going out?"

"Galleys normally come in long sheets, three pages or so to the sheet. For reviewers and people from whom we might wish to get a favorable quote for promotional purposes, we cut the galleys and bind them in cheap cardboard covers and send them out." Ticknor seemed more at ease now, with the third martini half inside him. I was still fighting off the peanuts.

"You have a list of people to whom you send these?"

Ticknor nodded. "I can get it to you tomorrow."

"Okay. Now, after the galleys went out, came the phone-calls. Tell me about them."

She was eating her martini olive. Her teeth were small and even and looked well cared-for. "A man's voice," she said. "He called me a dyke, 'a fucking dyke,' as I recall. And told me if that book was published, I'd be dead the day it hit the streets."

"Books don't hit the streets," I said. "Newspapers do. The idiot can't get his clichés straight."

"There has been a call like that every day for the last week."

"Always say the same thing?"

"Not word for word, but approximately. The substance is always that I'll die if the book is published."

"Same voice all the time?"

"No."

"That's too bad."

Ticknor said, "Why?"

"Makes it seem less like a single cuckoo getting his rocks off on the phone," I said. "I assume you've rejected the idea of withdrawing the book."

Rachel Wallace said, "Absolutely."

Ticknor said, "We suggested that. We said we'd not hold her to the contract."

"You also mentioned returning the advance," Rachel Wallace said.

"We run a business, Rachel."

"So do I," she said. "My business is with women's rights and with gay liberation and with writing." She looked at me. "I cannot let them frighten me. I cannot let them stifle me. Do you understand that?"

I said yes.

"That's your job," she said. "To see that I'm allowed to speak."

"What is there in the new book," I said, "that would cause people to kill you?"

"It began as a book about sexual prejudice. Discrimination in the job market against women, gay people, and specifically gay women. But it has expanded. Sexual prejudice goes hand in hand with other forms of corruption. Violation of the equal employment laws is often accompanied by violation of other laws. Bribery, kickbacks, racket tie-ins. I have named names as I found them. A lot of people will be hurt by my book. All of them deserve it."

"Corporations," Ticknor said, "local government agencies, politicians, city hall, the Roman Catholic Church. She has taken on a lot of the local power structure."

"Is it all Greater Boston?"

"Yes," she said. "I use it as a microcosm. Rather than trying to generalize about the nation, I study one large city very closely. Synecdoche, the rhetoricians would call it."

"Yeah," I said, "I bet they would."

"So," Ticknor said, "you see there are plenty of potential villains."

"May I have a copy of the book to read?"

"I brought one along," Ticknor said. He took his briefcase off the floor, opened it, and took out a book with a green dust jacket. The title, in salmon letters, took up most of the front. Rachel Wallace's picture took up most of the back. "Just out," Ticknor said.

"I'll read it tonight," I said. "When do I report for work?"

"Right now," Rachel Wallace said. "You are here. You are armed. And quite frankly I have been frightened. I won't be deflected. But I am frightened."

"What are your plans for today?" I said.

"We shall have perhaps three more drinks here, then you and I shall go to dinner. After dinner I shall go to my room and work until midnight. At midnight I shall go to bed. Once I am in my room with the door locked, I should think you could leave. The security here is quite good, I'm sure. At the slightest rustle outside my door I will call the hotel security number without a qualm."

"And tomorrow?"

"Tomorrow you should meet me at my room at eight o'clock. I have a speech in the morning and an autographing in the afternoon."

"I have a date for dinner tonight," I said. "May I ask her to join us?"

"You're not married," she said.

"That's true," I said.

"Is this a casual date or is this your person?"

"It's my person," I said.

Ticknor said, "We can't cover her expenses, you know."

"Oh, damn," I said.

"Yes, of course, bring her along. I hope that you don't plan to cart her everywhere, however. Business and pleasure, you know."

"She isn't someone you cart," I said. "If she joins us, it will be your good fortune."

"I don't care for your tone, buster," Rachel Wallace said. "I have a perfectly legitimate concern that you will not be distracted by your lady friend from doing what we pay you to do. If there's danger, would you look after her first or me."

"Her," I said.

"Then certainly I can suggest that she not always be with us."

"She won't be," I said. "I doubt that she could stand it."

"Perhaps I shall change my mind about this evening," Rachel Wallace said.

"Perhaps I shall change mine, too," I said.

Ticknor said, "Wait. Now just wait. I'm sure Rachel meant no harm. Her point is valid. Surely, Spenser, you understand that."

I didn't say anything.

"Dinner this evening, of course, is perfectly understandable," Ticknor said. "You had a date. You had no way to know that Rachel would require you today. I'm sure Rachel will be happy to have dinner with you both."

Rachel Wallace didn't say anything.

"Perhaps you could call the lady and ask her to meet you."

Rachel Wallace didn't like Ticknor saying "lady," but she held back and settled for giving him a disgusted look. Which he missed, or ignored—I couldn't tell which.

"Where are we eating?" I said to Rachel.

"I'd like the best restaurant in town," she said. "Do you have a suggestion?"

"The best restaurant in town is not *in* town. It's in Marblehead, place called Rosalie's."

"What's the cuisine?"

"Northern Italian Eclectic. A lot of it is just Rosalie's."

"No meatball subs? No pizza?"

"No."

"Do you know this restaurant, John?"

"I've not been out there. I've heard that it is excellent."

"Very well, we'll go. Tell your friend that we shall meet her there at seven. I'll call for reservations."

"My friend is named Susan. Susan Silverman."

"Fine," Rachel Wallace said.

4

ROSALIE'S IS IN a renovated commercial building in one of the worst sections of Marblehead. But the worst section of Marblehead is upper middle class. The commercial building had probably once manufactured money clips.

The restaurant is up a flight and inside the door is a small stand-up bar. Susan was at the bar drinking a glass of Chablis and talking to a young man in a corduroy jacket and a plaid shirt. He had a guardsman's mustache twirled upward at the ends. I thought about strangling him with it.

We paused inside the door for a moment. Susan didn't see us, and Wallace was looking for the maître d'. Susan had on a double-breasted camel's-hair jacket and matching skirt. Under the jacket was a forest-green shirt open at the throat. She had on high boots that disappeared under the skirt. I always had the sense that when I came upon her suddenly in a slightly unusual setting, a pride of trumpets ought to play alarms and flourishes. I stepped up to the bar next to her and said, "I beg your pardon, but the very sight of you makes my heart sing like an April day on the wings of spring."

She turned toward me and smiled and said, "Everyone tells me that."

She gestured toward the young man with the guardsman's mustache. "This is Tom," she said. And then with the laughing touch of evil in her eyes she said, "Tom was nice enough to buy me a glass of Chablis."

I said to Tom, "That's *one*."

He said, "Excuse me?"

I said, "It's the tag line to an old joke. Nice to meet you."

"Yeah," Tom said, "same here."

The maître d', in a dark velvet three-piece suit, was standing with Rachel Wallace. I said, "Bring your wine and come along."

She smiled at Tom and we stepped over to Wallace. "Rachel Wallace," I said, "Susan Silverman."

Susan put out her hand. "Hi, Rachel," she said. "I think your books are wonderful."

Wallace smiled, took her hand, and said, "Thank you. Nice to meet you."

The maître d' led us to our table, put the menus in front of us, and said, "I'll have someone right over to take your cocktail order."

I sat across from Susan, with Rachel Wallace on my left. She was a pleasant-looking woman, but next to Susan she looked as if she'd been washed in too much bleach. She was a tough, intelligent national figure, but next to Susan I felt sorry for her. On the other hand I felt sorry for all women next to Susan.

Rachel said, "Tell me about Spenser. Have you known him long?"

"I met him in 1973," Susan said, "but I've known him forever."

"It only seems like forever," I said, "when I'm talking."

Rachel ignored me. "And what is he like?"

"He's like he seems," Susan said. The waitress came and took our cocktail order.

"No, I mean in detail, what is he like? I am perhaps dependent on him to protect my life. I need to know about him."

"I don't like to say this in front of him, but for that you could have no one better."

"Or as good," I said.

"You've got to overcome this compulsion to understate your virtues," Susan said. "You're too self-effacing."

"Can he suspend his distaste for radical feminism enough to protect me properly?"

Susan looked at me and widened her eyes. "Hadn't you better answer that, snookie?" she said.

"You're begging the question, I think. We haven't established my distaste for radical feminism. We haven't even in fact established that you are a radical feminist."

"I have learned," Rachel Wallace said, "to assume a distaste for radical feminism. I rarely err in that."

"Probably right," I said.

"He's quite a pain in the ass, sometimes," Susan said. "He knows you want him to reassure you and he won't. But I will. He doesn't much care about radical feminism one way or the other. But if he says he'll protect you, he will."

"I'm not being a pain in the ass," I said. "Saying I have no distaste for her won't reassure her. Or it shouldn't. There's no way to prove anything to her until something happens. Words don't do it."

"Words can," Susan said. "And tone of voice. You're just so goddamned autonomous that you won't explain yourself to anybody."

The waitress came back with wine for Susan and Beck's beer for me, and another martini for Rachel Wallace. The five she'd had this afternoon seemed to have had no effect on her.

"Maybe I shouldn't cart her around everyplace," I said to Rachel.

"Machismo," Rachel said. "The machismo code. He's locked into it, and he can't explain himself, or apologize, or cry probably, or show emotion."

"I throw up good, though. And I will in a minute."

Wallace's head snapped around at me. Her face was harsh and tight. Susan patted her arm. "Give him time," she said. "He grows on you. He's hard to classify. But he'll look out for you. And he'll care what happens to you. And he'll keep you out of harm's way." Susan sipped her wine. "He really will," she said to Rachel Wallace.

"And you," Rachel said, "does he look out for you?"

"We look out for each other," Susan said. "I'm doing it now."

Rachel Wallace smiled, her face loosened. "Yes," she said. "You are, aren't you?"

The waitress came again, and we ordered dinner.

I was having a nice time eating Rosalie's cream of carrot soup when Rachel Wallace said, "John tells me you used to be a prizefighter."

I nodded. I had a sense where the discussion would lead.

"And you were in combat in Korea?"

I nodded again.

"And you were a policeman?"

Another nod.

"And now you do this."

It was a statement. No nod required.

"Why did you stop fighting?"

"I had plateaued," I said.

"Were you not a good fighter?"

"I was good. I was not great. Being a good fighter is no life. Only great ones lead a life worth too much. It's not that clean a business, either."

"Did you tire of the violence?"

"Not in the ring," I said.

"You didn't mind beating someone bloody."

"He volunteered. The gloves are padded. It's not pacifism, but if it's violence, it is controlled and regulated and patterned. I never hurt anyone badly. I never got badly hurt."

"Your nose has obviously been broken."

"Many times," I said. "But that's sort of minor. It hurts, but it's not serious."

"And you've killed people."

"Yes."

"Not just in the army."

"No."

"What kind of a person does that?" she said.

Susan was looking very closely at some of the decor in Rosalie's. "That is a magnificent old icechest," she said. "Look at the brass hinges."

"Don't change the subject for him," Rachel Wallace said. "Let him answer."

She spoke a little sharply for my taste. But if there was

anything sure on this earth, it was that Susan could take care of herself. She was hard to overpower.

"Actually," she said, "I was changing the subject for me. You'd be surprised at how many times I've heard this conversation."

"You mean we are boring you."

Susan smiled at her. "A tweak," she said.

"I bore a lot of people," Rachel said. "I don't mind. I'm willing to be boring to find out what I wish to know."

The waitress brought me veal Giorgio. I ate a bite.

"What is it you want to know?"

"Why you engage in things that are violent and dangerous."

I sipped half a glass of beer. I took another bite of veal. "Well," I said, "the violence is a kind of side-effect, I think. I have always wanted to live life on my own terms. And I have always tried to do what I can do. I am good at certain kinds of things; I have tried to go in that direction."

"The answer doesn't satisfy me," Rachel said.

"It doesn't have to. It satisfies me."

"What he won't say," Susan said, "and what he may not even admit to himself is that he'd like to be Sir Gawain. He was born five hundred years too late. If you understand that, you understand most of what you are asking."

"Six hundred years," I said.

5

WE GOT THROUGH the rest of dinner. Susan asked Rachel about her books and her work, and that got her off me and onto something she liked much better. Susan is good at that. After dinner I had to drive Rachel back to the Ritz. I said goodbye to Susan in the bank parking lot behind Rosalie's where we'd parked.

"Don't be mean to her," Susan said softly. "She's scared to death, and she's badly ill at ease with you and with her fear."

"I don't blame her for being scared," I said. "But it's not my fault."

From the front seat of my car Rachel said, "Spenser, I have work to do."

"Jesus Christ," I said to Susan.

"She's scared," Susan said. "It makes her bitchy. Think how you'd feel if she were your only protection."

I gave Susan a pat on the fanny, decided a kiss would be

hokey, and opened the door for her before she climbed into her MG. I was delighted. She'd gotten rid of the Nova. She was not Chevy. She was sports car.

Through the open window Susan said, "You held the door just to spite her."

"Yeah, baby, but I'm going home with her."

Susan slid into gear and wheeled the sports car out of the lot. I got in beside Rachel and started up my car.

"For heaven's sake, what year is this car?" Rachel said.

"1968," I said. "I'd buy a new one, but they don't make convertibles anymore." Maybe I should get a sports car. Was I old Chevy?

"Susan is a very attractive person," Rachel said.

"That's true," I said.

"It makes me think better of you that she likes you."

"That gets me by in a lot of places," I said.

"Your affection for each other shows."

I nodded.

"It is not my kind of love, but I can respond to it in others. You are lucky to have a relationship as vital as that."

"That's true, too," I said.

"You don't like me."

I shrugged.

"You don't," she said.

"It's irrelevant," I said.

"You don't like me, and you don't like what I stand for."

"What is it you stand for?" I said.

"The right of every woman to be what she will be. To shape her life in conformity to her own impulse, not to bend her will to the whims of men."

I said, "Wow."

"Do you realize I bear my father's name?"

"I didn't know that," I said.

"I had no choice," she said. "It was assigned me."

"That's true of me, too," I said.

She looked at me.

"It was assigned me. Spenser. I had no choice. I couldn't say I'd rather be named Spade. Samuel Spade. That would have been a terrific name, but no. I had to get a name like an English poet. You know what Spenser wrote?"

"*The Faerie Queen*?"

"Yeah. So what are you bitching about?"

We were out of Marblehead now and driving on Route 1A through Swampscott.

"It's not the same," she said.

"Why isn't it?"

"Because I'm a woman and was given a man's name."

"Whatever name would have been without your consent. Your mother's, your father's, and if you'd taken your mother's name, wouldn't that merely have been your grandfather's?"

There was a blue Buick Electra in front of me. It began to slow down as we passed the drive-in theater on the Lynnway. Behind me a Dodge swung out into the left lane and pulled up beside me.

"Get on the floor," I said.

She said, "What—" and I put my right hand behind her neck and pushed her down toward the floor. With my left hand I yanked the steering wheel hard over and went inside the Buick. My right wheels went up on the curb. The Buick pulled right to crowd me, and I floored the Chevy and dragged my bumper along his entire righthand side and spun off the curb in front of him with a strong smell of skun rubber behind me. I went up over the General Edwards Bridge with the accelerator to the floor and my elbow on the horn, and with the Buick and the Dodge behind me. I had my elbow on the horn because I had my gun in my hand.

The Lynnway was too bright and too busy, and it was too early in the evening. The Buick swung off into Point of Pines, and the Dodge went with it. I swerved into the passing lane to avoid a car and swerved back to the right to avoid another and began to slow down.

Rachel Wallace crouched, half fetal, toward the floor on the passenger's side. I put the gun down on the seat beside me. "One of the advantages of driving a 1968 Chevy," I said, "is you don't care all that much about an occasional dent."

"May I sit up?" she said. Her voice was strong.

"Yeah."

She squirmed back up onto the seat.

"Was that necessary?"

"Yeah."

"Was there someone really chasing us?"

"Yeah."

"If there was, you handled it well. My reactions would not have been as quick."

I said, "Thank you."

"I'm not complimenting you. I'm merely observing a fact. Did you get their license numbers?"

"Yes, 469AAG, and D60240, both Mass. But it won't do us any good unless they are bad amateurs, and the way they boxed me on the road before I noticed, they aren't amateurs."

"You think you should have noticed them sooner?"

"Yeah. I was too busy arguing patristic nomenclature with you. I should never have had to hit the curb like that."

"Then partly it is my fault for distracting you."

"It's not your line of work. It is mine. You don't know better. I do."

"Well," she said, "no harm done. We got away."

"If the guy in front of us in the Buick was just a mohair better, we wouldn't have."

"He would have cut you off?"

I nodded. "And the Dodge would have blasted us."

"Actually would he not have blasted you? I was on the floor, and you were much closer anyway."

I shrugged. "It wouldn't have mattered. If you survived the crash they'd have waited and blasted you."

"You seem, so, so at ease with all of this."

"I'm not. It scares me."

"Perhaps. It scares me, too. But you seem to expect it. There's no moral outrage. You're not appalled. Or offended. Or . . . aghast. I don't know. You make this seem so commonplace."

"*Aghast* is irrelevant, too. It's useless. Or expressing it is useless. On the other hand I'm not one of the guys in the other car."

We went past the dog track and around Bell Circle. There was no one noticeable in the rearview mirror.

"Then you do what you do in part from moral outrage."

I looked at her and shook my head. "I do what I do because I'm comfortable doing it."

"My God," she said, "you're a stubborn man."

"Some consider it a virtue in my work," I said.

She looked at the gun lying on the seat.

"Oughtn't you to put that away?"

"I think I'll leave it there till we get to the Ritz."

"I've never touched a gun in my life."

"They're a well-made apparatus," I said. "If they're good. Very precise."

"Is this good?"

"Yes. It's a very nice gun."

"No gun is nice," she said.

"If those gentlemen from the Lynnway return," I said, "you may come to like it better."

She shook her head. "It's come to that. Sometimes I feel sick thinking about it."

"What?"

"In this country—the land of the free and all that shit—I need a man with a gun to protect me simply because I am what I am."

"That's fairly sickening," I said.

6

I PICKED RACHEL WALLACE up at her door at eight thirty the next morning, and we went down to breakfast in the Ritz Café. I was wearing my bodyguard outfit—jeans, T-shirt, corduroy Levi jacket, and a daring new pair of Pumas: royal-blue suede with a bold gold stripe. Smith and Wesson .38 Police Special in a shoulder holster.

Rachel Wallace said, "Well, we are somewhat less formal this morning, aren't we? If you're dressed that way tonight, they won't let you in the dining room."

"Work clothes," I said. "I can move well in them."

She nodded and ate an egg. She wore a quiet gray dress with a paisley scarf at her throat. "You expect to have to move?"

"Probably not," I said. "But like they say at the Pentagon, you have to plan for the enemy's capacity, not his intentions."

She signed the check. "Come along," she said. She picked

up her briefcase from under the table, and we walked out through the lobby. She got her coat from the check room, a pale tan trenchcoat. It had cost money. I made no effort to hold it for her. She ignored me while she put it on. I looked at the lobby. There were people, but they looked like they belonged there. No one had a Gatling gun. At least no one had one visible. In fact I'd have been the only one I would have been suspicious of if I hadn't known me so well, and so fondly.

A young woman in a green tweed suit and a brown beret came toward us from the Arlington Street entrance.

"Ms. Wallace. Hi. I've got a car waiting."

"Do you know her?" I said.

"Yes," Rachel said. "Linda Smith."

"I mean by sight," I said. "Not just by hearing of her or getting mail from her."

"Yes, we've met several times before."

"Okay."

We went out onto Arlington Street. I went first. The street was normal nine AM busy. There was a tan Volvo sedan parked at the yellow curb with the motor running and the doorman standing with his hand on the passenger door. When he saw Linda Smith, he opened the passenger door. I looked inside the car and then stepped aside. Rachel Wallace got in; the doorman closed the door. I got in the back, and Linda Smith got in the driver's seat.

As we pulled into traffic Rachel said, "Have you met Mr. Spenser, Linda?"

"No, I haven't. Nice to meet you, Mr. Spenser."

"Nice to meet you, Ms. Smith," I said. Rachel would like the *Ms.*

"Spenser is looking after me on the tour," Rachel said.

"Yes, I know. John told me." She glanced at me in the rearview mirror. "I don't think I've ever met a bodyguard before."

"We're just regular folks," I said. "If you cut us, do we not bleed?"

"Literary, too," Linda Smith said.

"When are we supposed to be in Belmont?"

"Ten o'clock," Linda said. "Belmont Public Library."

"What for?" I said.

"Ms. Wallace is speaking there. They have a Friends of the Library series."

"Nice liberal town you picked."

"Never mind, Spenser," Rachel Wallace said. Her voice was brusque. "I told them I'd speak wherever I could and to whom I could. I have a message to deliver, and I'm not interested in persuading those who already agree with me."

I nodded.

"If there's trouble, all right. That's what you're being paid for."

I nodded.

We got to the Belmont Library at a quarter to ten. There were ten men and women walking up and down in front of the library with placards on poles made of strapping.

A Belmont Police cruiser was parked across the street, two cops sitting in it quietly.

"Park behind the cops," I said.

Linda swung in behind the cruiser, and I got out. "Stay in the car a second," I said.

"I will not cower in here in front of a few pickets."

"Then look menacing while you sit there. This is what I'm paid for. I just want to talk to the cops."

I walked over to the cruiser. The cop at the wheel had a

young wise-guy face. He looked like he'd tell you to stick it, at the first chance he got. And laugh. He was chewing a toothpick, the kind they put through a club sandwich. It still had the little cellophane frill on the end he wasn't chewing.

I bent down and said through the open window, "I'm escorting this morning's library speaker. Am I likely to have any trouble from the pickets?"

He looked at me for ten or twelve seconds, worrying the toothpick with his tongue.

"You do, and we'll take care of it," he said. "You think we're down here waiting to pick up a copy of *Gone with the Wind*?"

"I figured you more for picture books," I said.

He laughed. "How about that, Benny?" he said to his partner. "A hot shit. Haven't had one today." His partner was slouched in the seat with his hat tipped over his eyes. He didn't say anything or move. "Who's the speaker you're escorting?"

"Rachel Wallace," I said.

"Never heard of her."

"I'll try to keep that from her," I said. "I'm going to take her in now."

"Good show," he said. "Shouldn't be any trouble for a hot shit like you."

I went back to the car and opened the door for Rachel Wallace.

"What did you do?" she said as she got out.

"Annoyed another cop," I said. "That's three hundred sixty-one this year, and October's not over yet."

"Did they say who the pickets were?"

I shook my head. We started across the street, Linda

Smith on one side of Rachel and me on the other. Linda Smith's face looked tight and colorless; Rachel's was expressionless.

Someone among the pickets said, "There she is." They all turned and closed together more tightly as we walked toward them. Linda looked at me, then back at the cops. We kept walking.

"We don't want you here!" a woman shouted at us.

Someone else yelled, "Dyke!"

I said, "Is he talking to me?"

Rachel Wallace said, "No."

A heavy-featured woman with shoulder-length gray hair was carrying a placard that said, A Gay America is a Communist Goal. A stylish woman in a tailored suit carried a sign that read, Gays Can't Reproduce. They Have to Convert.

I said, "I bet she wanted to say proselytize; but no one knew how to spell it."

No one laughed; I was getting used to that. As we approached the group they joined arms in front of us, blocking the entrance. In the center of the line was a large man with a square jaw and thick brown hair. Looked like he'd been a tight end perhaps, at Harvard. He wore a dark suit and a pale gray silk tie. His cheeks were rosy, and his eye was clear. Probably still active in his alumni association. A splendid figure of a man, the rock upon which the picket line was anchored. Surely a foe of atheism, Communism, and faggotry. Almost certainly a perfect asshole.

Rachel Wallace walked directly up to him and said, "Excuse me, please."

There was no shouting now. It was quiet. Square Jaw shook his head, slowly, dramatically.

Rachel said, "You are interfering with my right of free speech and free assembly, a right granted me by the Constitution."

Nobody budged. I looked back at the cops. The wise-guy kid was out of the squad car now, leaning against the door on the passenger side, his arms crossed, his black leather belt sagging with ammunition, Mace, handcuffs, nightstick, gun, come-along, and a collection of keys on a ring. He probably wanted to walk over and let us through, but his gunbelt was too heavy.

I said to Rachel, "Would you like me to create an egress for you?"

"How do you propose to do it," she said.

"I thought I would knock this matinee idol on his kiester, and we could walk in over him."

"It might be a mistake to try, fellow," he said. His voice was full of money, like Daisy Buchanan.

"No," I said. "It would not be a mistake."

Rachel said, "Spenser." Her voice was sharp. "I don't stand for that," she said. "I won't resort to it."

I shrugged and looked over at the young cop. His partner appeared not to have moved. He was still sitting in the squad car with his hat over his eyes. Maybe it was an economy move; maybe the partner was really an inflatable dummy. The young cop grinned at me.

"Our civil rights are in the process of violation over here!" I yelled at him. "You have any plans for dealing with that?"

He pushed himself away from the car and swaggered over. His half-chewed toothpick bobbed in his mouth as he worked it back and forth with his tongue. The handle of his service revolver thumped against his leg. On his uniform blouse were several military service ribbons. Vietnam, I figured. There was a Purple Heart ribbon and a service ribbon with battle stars and another ribbon that might have been the Silver Star.

"You could look at it that way," he said when he reached us. "Or you could look at it that you people are causing a disturbance."

"Will you escort us inside, officer?" Rachel Wallace said. "I would say that is your duty, and I think you ought to do it."

"We are here to prevent the spreading of an immoral and pernicious doctrine, officer," Square Jaw said. "That is *our* duty. I do not think you should *aid* people who wish to destroy the American family."

The cop looked at Rachel.

"I will not be caught up in false issues," Rachel said. "We have a perfect right to go into that library and speak. I have been invited, and I will speak. There is no question of right here. I have a right and they are trying to violate it. Do your job."

Other people were gathering, passing cars slowed down and began to back up traffic while the drivers tried to see what was happening. On the fringes of the crowd post-high-school kids gathered and smirked.

Square Jaw said, "It might help you to keep in mind, officer, that I am a close personal friend of Chief Garner, and I'm sure he'll want to hear from me exactly what has happened and how his men have behaved."

The young cop looked at me. "A friend of the chief," he said.

"That's frightening," I said. "You better walk softly around him."

The young cop grinned at me broadly. "Yeah," he said. He turned back to Square Jaw. "Move it, Jack," he said. The smile was gone.

Square Jaw rocked back a little as if someone had jabbed at him.

"I beg your pardon?" he said.

"I said, Move your ass. This broad may be a creep, but she didn't try to scare me. I don't like people to try and scare me. These people are going in—you can tell the chief that when you see him. You can tell him they went in past you or over you. You decide which you'll tell him."

The young cop's face was half an inch away from Square Jaw's, and since he was three inches shorter, it was tilted up. The partner had appeared from the car. He was older and heavier, with a pot belly and large hands with big knuckles. He had his night stick in his right hand, and he slapped it gently against his thigh.

The people on either side of Square Jaw unlinked their arms and moved away. Square Jaw looked at Rachel, and when he spoke he almost hissed. "You foul, contemptible woman," he said. "You bulldyke. We'll never let you win. You queer . . ."

I pointed down the street to the left and said to the two cops, "There's trouble."

They both turned to look, and when they did I gave Square Jaw a six-inch jab in the solar plexus with my right fist. He gasped and doubled up. The cops spun back and looked at him and then at me. I was staring down the street where I'd pointed. "Guess I was mistaken," I said.

Square Jaw was bent over, his arms wrapped across his midsection, rocking back and forth. A good shot in the solar plexus will half-paralyze you for a minute or two.

The young cop looked at me without expression. "Yeah, I guess you were," he said. "Well let's get to the library."

As we walked past Square Jaw the older cop said to him, "It's a violation of health ordinances, Jack, to puke in the street."

7

INSIDE THE LIBRARY, and downstairs in the small lecture room, there was no evidence that a disturbance had ever happened. The collection of elderly people, mostly women, all gray-haired, mostly overweight, was sitting placidly on folding chairs, staring patiently at the small platform and the empty lectern.

The two cops left us at the door. "We'll sit around outside," the young one said, "until you're through." Rachel Wallace was being introduced to the Friends of the Library president, who would introduce her to the audience. The young cop looked at her. "What did you say her name was?"

"Rachel Wallace," I said.

"She some kind of queer or something?"

"She's a writer," I said. "She's a feminist. She's gay. She's not easy to scare."

The cop shook his head, "A goddamned lezzy," he said to his partner. "We'll be outside," he said to me. They started up the stairs. Three steps up the young cop stopped and turned back to me. "You got a good punch," he said. "You don't see a lot of guys can hit that hard on a short jab." Then he turned and went on up after his partner. Inside the room Rachel Wallace was sitting on a folding chair beside the lectern, her hands folded in her lap, her ankles crossed. The president was introducing her. On a table to the right of the lectern were maybe two dozen of Rachel Wallace's books. I leaned against the wall to the right of the door in the back and looked at the audience. No one looked furtive. Not all of them looked awake. Linda Smith was standing next to me.

"Nice booking," I said to her.

She shrugged. "It all helps," she said. "Did you hit that man outside?"

"Just once," I said.

"I wonder what she'll say about that," Linda Smith said.

I shrugged.

The president finished introducing Rachel and she stepped to the lectern. The audience clapped politely.

"I am here," Rachel said, "for the same reason I write. Because I have a truth to tell, and I will tell it."

I whispered to Linda Smith, "You think many of these people have read her books?"

Linda shook her head. "Most of them just like to come out and look at a real live author."

"The word *woman* is derived from the Old English *wifmann* meaning 'wife-person.' The very noun by which our language designates us does so only in terms of men."

The audience looked on loyally and strained to understand. Looking at them, you'd have to guess that the majority of them couldn't find any area where they could agree with her. At least a plurality probably couldn't find an area where they understood what she was talking about. They were library friends, people who had liked to read all their lives, and liked it in the library and had a lot of free time on their hands. Under other circumstances they would have shot a lesbian on sight.

"I am not here," Rachel Wallace was saying, "to change your sexual preference. I am here only to say that sexual preference is not a legitimate basis for discriminatory practices, for maltreatment in the marketplace. I am here to say that a woman can be fulfilled without a husband and children, that a woman is not a breeding machine, that she need not be a slave to her family, a whore for her husband."

An elderly man in a gray sharkskin suit leaned over to his wife and whispered something. Her shoulders shook with silent laughter. A boy about four years old got up from his seat beside his grandmother and walked down the center aisle to sit on the floor in front and stare up at Rachel. In the very last row a fat woman in a purple dress read a copy of *Mademoiselle.*

"How many books does this sell?" I whispered to Linda Smith.

She shrugged. "There's no way to know, really," she whispered. "The theory is that exposure helps. The more the better. Big scenes like the *Today Show*, small ones like this. You try to blanket a given area."

"Are there any questions?" Rachel said. The audience stared at her. A man wearing white socks and bedroom slippers was asleep in the front row, right corner. In the silence the pages turning in *Mademoiselle* were loud. The woman didn't seem to notice.

"If not, then thank you very much."

Rachel stepped off the low platform past the small boy and walked down the center aisle toward Linda and me. Outside the hall there were multicolored small cookies on a table and a large coffee maker with a thumbprint near the spigot. Linda said to Rachel, "That was wonderful."

Rachel said, "Thank you."

The president of the Friends said, "Would you like some coffee and refreshments?"

Rachel said, "No, thank you." She jerked her head at me, and the three of us headed for the door.

"You sure you don't want any refreshment?" I said, as we went out the side door of the library.

"I want two maybe three martinis and lunch," Rachel said. "What have I this afternoon, Linda?"

"An autographing in Cambridge."

Rachel shivered. "God," she said.

There was no one outside now except the two cops in the squad car. The pickets were gone, and the lawn was empty and innocent in front of the library. I shot at the young cop with my forefinger and thumb as we got into Linda Smith's car. He nodded. We drove away.

"You and the young officer seem to have developed some sort of relationship. Have you met him before?"

"Not him specifically, but we know some of the same things. When I was his age, I was sort of like him."

"No doubt," she said, without any visible pleasure. "What sort of things do you both know? And how do you know you know them?"

I shrugged. "You wouldn't get it, I don't think. I don't even know how we know, but we do."

"Try," Rachel said. "I am not a dullard. Try to explain."

"We know what hurts," I said, "and what doesn't. We know about being scared and being brave. We know applied theory."

"You can tell that, just by looking?"

"Well, partly. He had some combat decorations on his blouse."

"Military medals?"

"Yeah, cops sometimes wear them. He does. He's proud of them."

"And that's the basis of your judgment?"

"No, not just that. It's the way he walks. How his mouth looks, the way he holds his head. The way he reacted to the protest leader."

"I thought him a parody of machismo."

"No, not a parody," I said. "The real thing."

"The real thing is a parody," she said.

"I didn't think you'd get it," I said.

"Don't you patronize me," she said. "Don't use that oh-women-don't-understand-tone with me."

"I said you didn't understand. I didn't say other women don't. I didn't say it was because you're a woman."

"And," she snapped, "I assume you think you were some kind of Sir Galahad protecting my good name when you punched that poor sexist fool at the library. Well, you were not. You were a stupid thug. I will not have you acting on my behalf in a manner I deplore. If you strike another person except to save my life, I will fire you at that moment."

"How about if I stick my tongue out at them and go *bleaaah.*"

"I'm serious," she said.

"I'll say."

We were perfectly quiet then. Linda Smith drove back through Watertown toward Cambridge.

"I really thought the talk went very well, Rachel," she said. "That was a tough audience, and I thought you really got to them."

Rachel Wallace didn't answer.

"I thought we could go into Cambridge and have lunch at the Harvest," Linda said. "Then we could stroll up to the bookstore."

"Good," Rachel said. "I'm hungry, and I need a drink."

8

IN MY MOUTH there was still the faint taste of batter-fried shrimp with mustard fruits as I hung around the front door of the Crimson Book Store on Mass. Ave. and watched Rachel Wallace sign books. Across the street Harvard Yard glistened in the fall rain that had started while we were eating lunch.

Rachel was at a card table near the check-out counter in the front of the store. On the card table were about twenty copies of her new book and three blue felt-tipped pens. In the front window a large sign announced that she'd be there from one until three that day. It was now two ten, and they had sold three books. Another half dozen people had come in and looked at her and gone out.

Linda Smith hung around the table and drank coffee and steered an occasional customer over. I looked at everyone who came in and learned nothing at all. At two fifteen a teenage girl came in wearing Levi's and a purple warmup jacket that said Brass Kaydettes on it.

"You really an author?" she said to Rachel.

Rachel said, "Yes, I am."

"You write this book?"

"Yes."

Linda Smith said, "Would you like to buy one? Ms. Wallace will autograph a copy."

The girl ignored her. "This book any good?" she said.

Rachel Wallace smiled. "I think so," she said.

"What's it about?"

"It's about being a woman and about the way people discriminate against women, and about the way that corruption leads to other corruption."

"Oh, yeah? Is it exciting?"

"Well, I wouldn't, ah, I wouldn't say it was exciting, exactly. It is maybe better described as powerful."

"I was thinking of being a writer," the kid said.

Rachel's smile was quite thin. "Oh, really?"

"Where do you get your ideas?"

"I think them up," Rachel said. The smile was so thin it was hard to see.

"Oh, yeah?" The girl picked up a copy of Rachel's book and looked at it, and turned it over and looked at the back. She read the jacket flap for a minute, then put the book down.

"This a novel?" the girl said.

"No," Rachel said.

"It's long as a novel."

"Yes," Rachel said.

"So why ain't it a novel?"

"It's nonfiction."

"Oh."

The girl's hair was leaf-brown and tied in two pigtails that lapped over her ears. She had braces on her teeth. She picked the book up again and flipped idly through the pages. There was silence.

Rachel Wallace said, "Are you thinking of buying a copy?"

The girl shook her head. "Naw," she said, "I got no money anyway."

"Then put the book down and go somewhere else," Rachel said.

"Hey, I ain't doing any harm," the girl said.

Rachel looked at her.

"Oh, I'm through anyway," the girl said and left the store.

"You got some smooth way with the reading public," I said.

"Little twerp," Rachel said. "Where do I get my ideas? Jesus Christ, where does she think I get them? Everyone asks me that. The question is inane."

"She probably doesn't know any better," I said.

Rachel Wallace looked at me and said nothing. I didn't have a sense that she thought me insightful.

Two young men came in. One was small and thin with a crew cut and gold-rimmed glasses. He had on a short yellow slicker with a hood up and blue serge pants with cuffs that stopped perhaps two inches above the tops of his wing-tipped cordovan shoes. He had rubbers on over the shoes. The other one was much bigger. He had the look of a fat weightlifter. He couldn't have been more than twenty-five, but he was starting to get bald. He wore a red-and-black plaid flannel shirt, a black down vest, and chino pants rolled up over laced work boots. The sleeves of his shirt were turned up.

The small one carried a white cardboard pastry box. I edged a little closer to Rachel when they came in. They didn't look bookstorish. As they stopped in front of Rachel's table I put my hand inside my jacket on the butt of my gun. As the small one opened the pastry box I moved. He came out with a chocolate cream pie and had it halfway into throwing position when I hit him with my shoulder. He got it off, side-armed and weakly, and it hit Rachel in the chest. I had the gun out now, and when the fat one grabbed at me I hit him on the wrist with the barrel. The small one bowled over backwards and fell on the floor.

I said, "Everybody freeze," and pointed my gun at them. Always a snappy line.

The fat one was clutching his wrist against his stomach. "It was only a freaking pie, man," he said.

The small one had scrunched up against the wall by the door. The wind was knocked out of him, and he was working on getting it back. I looked at Rachel. The pie had hit her on the left breast and slid down her dress to her lap, leaving a wide trail of chocolate and whipped cream.

I said to the men, "Roll over on the floor, face down. Clasp your hands back of your head."

The little one did what I said. His breath was back. The fat one said, "Hey, man, I think you broke my freaking wrist."

"On the floor," I said.

He went down. I knelt behind them and searched them quickly with my left hand, keeping the gun clear in my right. They had no weapons.

The bookstore manager and Linda Smith were busy with

paper towels trying to wipe the chocolate cream off Rachel; customers gathered in a kind of hushed circle—not frightened, embarrassed rather. I stood up.

Rachel's face was flushed, and her eyes were bright. "Sweets for the sweet, my dear," I said.

"Call the police," she said.

"You want to prefer charges?" I said.

"Absolutely," she said. "I want these two boars charged with assault."

From the floor the fat one said, "Aw, lady, it was only a freaking pie."

"Shut up," she said. "Shut your foul, stupid mouth now. You grunting ass. I will do everything I can to put you in jail for this."

I said, "Linda, could you call the buttons for us?"

She nodded and went over to the telephone behind the counter.

Rachel turned and looked at the five customers and two clerks in a small semicircle looking uncomfortable.

"What are you people looking at?" she said. "Go about your business. Go on. Move."

They began to drift away. All five customers went out. The two clerks went back to arranging books on a display table downstairs.

"I think this autographing is over," Rachel said.

"Yeah," I said, "but the cops are coming. You gotta wait for them. They get grouchy as hell when you call them and screw."

Linda Smith hung up the phone. "They'll be right along," she said.

And they were—a prowl car with two cops in uniform. They wanted to see my license and my gun permit, and they shook down both the assault suspects routinely and thoroughly. I didn't bother to tell them I'd already done it; they'd have done it again anyway.

"You want to prefer assault charges against these two, lady?" one of the prowlies said.

"My name is Rachel Wallace. And I certainly do."

"Okay, Rachel," the cop said. There was a fine network of red veins in each cheek. "We'll take them in. Sergeant's gonna like this one, Jerry. Assault with a pie."

They herded the two young men toward the door. The fat one said, "Geez, lady, it was just a freaking pie."

Rachel leaned toward him a little and said to him very carefully, "Eat a shit sandwich."

9

We drove back to the Ritz in silence. The traffic wasn't heavy yet, and Linda Smith didn't have to concentrate on driving as much as she did. As we went over the Mass. Ave. Bridge I looked at the way the rain dimpled the surface of the river. The sweep of the Charles from the bridge down toward the basin was very fine from the Mass. Ave. Bridge—much better when you walked across it, but okay from a car. The red-brick city on Beacon Hill, the original one, was prominent from here, capped by the gold dome of the Bulfinch State House. The high-rises of the modern city were all around it, but from here they didn't dominate. It was like looking back through the rain to the way it was, and maybe should have been.

Linda Smith turned off Mass. Ave. and onto Commonwealth. "You don't think I should have preferred charges," Rachel said to me.

"Not my business to think about that," I said.

"But you disapprove."

I shrugged. "Tends to clog up the court system."

"Was I to let them walk away after insulting and degrading me?"

"I could have kicked each one in the fanny," I said.

"That's your solution to everything," she said, and looked out the window.

"No, but it's a solution to some things. You want them punished. What do you think will happen to them. A night in jail and a fifty dollar fine, maybe. To get that done will involve two prowl-car cops, a desk sergeant, a judge, a prosecutor, a public defender, and probably more. It will cost the state about two thousand dollars, and you'll probably have to spend the morning in court and so will the two arresting officers. I could have made them sorry a lot sooner for free."

She continued to stare out the window.

"And," I said, "it was only a freaking pie, lady."

She looked at me and almost smiled. "You were very quick," she said.

"I didn't know it was going to be a pie."

"Would you have shot him?" she said. She wasn't looking out the window now; she stared straight at me.

"If I had to. I almost did before I saw it was a pie."

"What kind of a man would do that?"

"Throw a pie at someone?"

"No," she said. "Shoot someone."

"You asked me that before," I said. "I don't have a better answer this time except to say, Isn't it good you've got one? At the rate we're going, you'll be attacked by a horde of chauvinist cameldrivers before the week is out."

"You sound as if it were my fault. It is not. I do not cause trouble—I am beset by it because of my views."

Linda Smith pulled the car onto Arlington Street and into the open space in front of the Ritz. I said, "Stay in the car till I tell you."

I got out and looked both ways and into the lobby. The doorman hustled forward to open the door for Rachel. She looked at me. I nodded. She stepped out of the car and walked into the hotel.

"We'll have a drink in the bar," she said.

I nodded and followed her in. There were a couple of business types having Scotch on the rocks at a table by the window, and a college-age boy and girl sitting at another table, very dressed up and a little ill at ease. He had beer. She had a champagne cocktail. Or at least it looked like a champagne cocktail. I hoped it was.

Rachel slid onto a bar stool, and I sat next to her and turned my back to the bar and surveyed the room. No one but us and the business types and the college kids. Rachel's coat had a hood. She slid the hood off but kept the coat on to cover up the pie smear down the front of her dress.

"Beer, Spenser?"

"Yes, please."

She ordered. Beer for me and a martini for her. For the Ritz Bar I was spectacularly underdressed. I thought the bartender paled a little when I came in, but he said nothing and tended the bar just as if I were not offensive to his sight.

A young woman came into the bar alone. She had on a long cream-colored wool skirt and heavy black boots, the kind that seem to have extra leather. Her blouse was white.

There was a black silk scarf at her neck, and she carried a gray leather coat over her arm. Very stylish. The skirt fit well, I noticed, especially around the hips. She looked around the room and spotted us at the bar and came directly to us. The kid can still attract them, I thought. Still got the old whammo.

The young woman reached us and said, "Rachel," and put her hand out.

Rachel Wallace turned and looked at her and then smiled. She took the outstretched hand in both of hers. "Julie," she said. "Julie Wells." She leaned forward and Julie Wells put her face down and Rachel kissed her. "How lovely to see you," she said. "Sit down."

Julie slid onto the bar stool on the other side of Rachel.

"I heard you were in town again," she said, "and I knew you'd be staying here, so I got through work early and came over. I called your room, and when there was no answer, I thought, well, knowing Rachel, chances are she's in the bar."

"Well, you do know me," Rachel said. "Can you stay? Can you have dinner with me?"

"Sure," Julie said, "I was hoping you'd ask."

The bartender came over and looked questioningly at Julie. "I'll have a Scotch sour on the rocks," she said.

Rachel said, "I'll have another martini. Spenser, another beer?"

I nodded. The bartender moved away. Julie looked at me. I smiled at her. "We're on tour," I said. "Rachel plays the hand organ, and I go around with a little cup and collect money."

Julie said, "Oh, really," and looked at Rachel.

"His name is Spenser," Rachel said. "There have been

some threats about my new book. The publisher thought I should have a bodyguard. He thinks he's funny."

"Nice to meet you," Julie said.

"Nice to meet you, too," I said. "Are you an old friend of Rachel's?"

She and Rachel smiled at each other. "Sort of, I guess," Julie said. "Would you say so, Rachel?"

"Yes," Rachel said, "I would say that. I met Julie when I was up here doing the research for *Tyranny,* last year."

"You a writer, Julie?"

She smiled at me, very warm. *Zing* went the strings of my heart. "No," she said, "I wish I were. I'm a model."

"What agency?"

"Carol Cobb. Do you know the modeling business?"

"No, I'm just a curious person."

Rachel shook her head. "No, he's not," she said. "He's screening you. And I don't like it." She looked at me. "I appreciate that you have to do your job, and that today may have made you unduly suspicious. But Julie Wells is a close personal friend of mine. We have nothing to fear from her. I'll appreciate it if in the future you trust my judgment."

"Your judgment's not as good as mine," I said. "I have no involvement. How close a personal friend can someone be that you met only last year?"

"Spenser, that's enough," Rachel said. There was force in her voice and her face.

Julie said, "Rachel, I don't mind. Of course he has to be careful. I pray that he is. What are these threats? How serious are they?"

Rachel turned toward her. I sipped a little beer. "I've had phonecalls threatening me if *Tyranny* is published."

"But if you're on the promotion tour, it means it's been published already."

"In fact, yes, though technically publication date isn't until October fifteenth. The book is already in a lot of bookstores."

"Has anything happened?"

"There was an incident last night, and there have been protests. But I don't think they're related."

"The incident last night was the real goods," I said. "The other stuff was probably what it seemed."

"What happened last night?" Julie said.

"Spenser contends that someone tried to run us off the road last night in Lynn."

"Contends?" Julie said.

"Well, I was on the floor, and he swerved around a lot and then the car behind us was gone. I can't speak for sure myself. And if I were convinced no one were after me, Spenser would be out of work."

"Aw, you'd want me around anyway. All you chicks like a guy to look after you."

She threw her drink at me. She threw like a girl; most of it landed on my shirt front.

"Now we're both messy," I said. "A his-and-hers outfit."

The bartender slid down toward us. Julie put her hand on Rachel's arm. The bartender said, "Is there something wrong, ma'am?"

Rachel was silent. Her breath blew in and out through her nose.

I said to the bartender, "No, it's fine. She was kidding with me, and the drink slipped."

The bartender looked at me as if I were serious, smiled as if he believed me, and moved off down the bar. In maybe thirty seconds he was back with a new martini for Rachel. "This is on the house, ma'am," he said.

Julie said to me, "Why do you feel last night was serious?"

"It was professional," I said. "They knew what they were doing. We were lucky to get out of it."

"Rachel is hard sometimes," Julie said. She was patting the back of Rachel's left hand. "She doesn't mean everything she says and does always. Sometimes she regrets them, even."

"Me, too," I said. I wonder if I should pat the other hand. My T-shirt was wet against my chest, but I didn't touch it. It's like getting hit with a pitch. You're not supposed to rub.

Rachel said, "Julie and I will dine in our room tonight. I won't need you until tomorrow at eight."

"I better wait until Julie leaves," I said.

They both looked at me. Then Rachel said, "That's when she is going to leave."

I said, "Oh." Always the smooth comeback, even when I've been dumb. Of course they were very good friends.

"I'll walk up with you and hang around in the hall till the waiter has come and gone."

"That won't be necessary," Rachel said. She wouldn't look at me.

"Yeah, it will," I said. "I work at what I do, Rachel. I'm not going to let someone buzz you in the lobby just because you're mad at me."

She looked up at me. "I'm not mad at you," she said. "I'm ashamed of the way I behaved a moment ago."

Behind her Julie beamed at me. *See?* her smile said, *See? She's really very nice.*

"Either way," I said. "I'll stick around and wait till you've locked up for the night. I won't bother you—I'll lurk in the hall."

She nodded. "Perhaps that would be best," she said.

We finished our drinks, Rachel signed the bar tab, and we headed for the elevators. I went first; they followed. When we got in the elevator, Julie and Rachel were holding hands. The skirt still fit Julie's hips wonderfully. Was I a sexist? Was it ugly to think, *What a waste?* On Rachel's floor I got out first. The corridor was empty. At her room I took the key from Rachel and opened the door. The room was dark and silent. I went in and turned on the lights. There was no one there and no one in the bathroom. Rachel and Julie came in.

I said, "Okay, I'll say good night. I'll be in the hall. When room service comes, open the door on the chain first, and don't let him in unless I'm there, too. I'll come in with him."

Rachel nodded. Julie said, "Nice to have met you, Spenser."

I smiled at her and closed the door.

10

THE CORRIDOR WAS silent and Ritz-y, with gold-patterned wallpaper. I wondered if they'd make love before they ordered dinner. I would. I hoped they wouldn't. It had been a while since lunch and would be a long wait for dinner if it worked out wrong.

I leaned against the wall opposite their door. If they were making love, I didn't want to hear. The concept of love between two women didn't have much affect on me in the abstract. But if I imagined them at it, and speculated on exactly how they went about it, it seemed sort of too bad, demeaning. Actually maybe Susan and I weren't all that slick in the actual doing ourselves. When you thought about it, maybe none of us were doing Swan Lake. "What's right is what feels good afterwards," I said out loud in the empty corridor. Hemingway said that. Smart man, Hemingway. Spent very little time hanging around hotel corridors with no supper.

Down the corridor to my left a tall thin man with a black mustache and a double-breasted gray pinstripe suit came out of his room and past me, heading for the elevator. There was a silver pin in his collar under the modest knot of his tie. His black shoes glistened with polish. Class. Even more class than a wet Adidas T-shirt. The hell with him. He probably did not have a Smith and Wesson .38 caliber revolver with a four-inch barrel. And I did. *How's that for class?* I mumbled at his back as he went into the elevator.

About fifteen minutes later a housekeeper went bustling past me down the corridor and knocked on a door. No one answered, and the housekeeper let herself in with a key on a long chain. She was in for maybe a minute and came back past me and into the service elevator. She probably didn't have a .38 either.

I amused myself by trying to see how many lyrics I could sing to songs written by Johnny Mercer. I was halfway through "Memphis in June" when a pleasant-looking gray-haired man with a large red nose got out of the elevator and walked down the corridor toward me. He had on gray slacks and a blue blazer. On the blazer pocket was a small name plate that said Asst. Mgr.

His blazer also hung funny over his right hip, the way it does when you are carrying a gun in a hip holster. He smiled as he approached me. I noticed that the blazer was unbuttoned and his left hand was in a half fist. He sort of tapped it against his thigh, knuckles toward me.

"Are you locked out of your room, sir?" he said with a big smile. He was a big guy and had a big stomach, but he didn't look slow and he didn't look soft. His teeth had been capped.

I said, "House man, right?"

"Callahan," he said, "I'm the assistant night manager."

"Spenser," I said. "I'm going to take out my wallet and show you some ID."

"You're not registered here, Mr. Spenser."

"No, I'm working. I'm looking out for Rachel Wallace, who is registered here."

I handed him my license. He looked at it and looked at me. "Nice picture," he said.

"Well, that's my bad side," I said.

"It's full face," he said.

"Yeah," I said.

"Do I detect a weapon of some sort under your left arm, Mr. Spenser?"

"Yes. It makes us even—you got one on your right hip."

He smiled again. His half-clenched left fist tapped against his thigh.

"I'm in kind of a puzzle, Mr. Spenser. If you really are guarding Miss Wallace, I can't very well ask you to leave. On the other hand you could be lying. I guess we better ask her."

"Not right now," I said. "I think she's busy."

" 'Fraid we'll have to anyway."

"How do I know you're really the house dick?"

"Assistant manager," he said. "Says so right on my coat."

"Anyone can get a coat. How do I know this isn't a ploy to get her to open the door?"

He rolled his lower lip out. "Got a point there," he said. "What we do is go down the end of the hall by the elevators and call on the house phone. You can see the whole corridor and I can see you that way."

I nodded. We walked down to the phone side by side, watching each other and being careful. I was paying most attention to the half-closed fist. For a man his size it was a small fist. At the phones he tucked the phone between his cheek and shoulder and dialed with his right hand. He knew the number without looking. She took a long while to answer.

"Sorry to bother you, Miss Wallace. . . . Ms. Wallace. . . . Yeah. . . . Well, this is Callahan, the assistant manager. Do you have a man named Spenser providing personal security for you? . . . Unh-huh. . . . Describe him to me, if you would. . . . No, we just spotted him outside your room and thought we'd better check. . . . Yes, ma'am. Yes, that'll be fine. Thank you." He hung up.

"Okay," he said with a big friendly smile. "She validated you." He put his left hand into the side pocket of his blazer and took it out.

"What did you have in your hand?" I said. "Roll of quarters?"

"Dimes," he said. "Got a small hand."

"Who whistled on me—the housekeeper."

He nodded.

I said, "Are you looking out for Ms. Wallace special?"

"We're a little special on her," he said. "Got a call from a homicide dick said there'd been threats on her life."

"Who called you—Quirk?"

"Yeah, know him?"

I nodded.

"Friend of his?"

"I wouldn't go that far," I said.

We walked back down the corridor toward Rachel's room. "Good cop," Callahan said.

I nodded. "Very tough," I said.

"So I hear. I hear he's as tough as there is in this town."

"Top three," I said.

"Who else?"

"Guy named Hawk," I said. "He ever shows up in your hotel, don't try to take him with a roll of dimes."

"Who's the third?"

I smiled at him and ducked my head. "Aw, hell," I said.

He did his big friendly smile again. "Well, good we don't have to find that out," he said. His voice was steady. He seemed able to repress his terror. "Not tonight anyway." He nodded at me. "Have a good day," he said, and moved off placidly down the corridor. I must have frightened him to death.

I went back to my Johnny Mercer lyrics. I was on the third verse of "Midnight Sun" when a room service waiter came off the elevator pushing a table. He stopped at Rachel's door and knocked. He smiled at me as he waited. The door opened on the chain and a small vertical plane of Rachel Wallace's face appeared.

I said, "It's okay, Rachel. I'm here." The waiter smiled at me again, as if I'd said something clever. The door closed and in a moment re-opened. The waiter went in, and I came in behind him. Rachel was in a dark-brown full-length robe with white piping. She wore no make-up. Julie Wells wasn't in the room. The bathroom door was closed, and I could hear the shower going. Both beds were a little rumpled but still made.

The waiter opened up the table and began to lay out the supper. I leaned against the wall by the window and watched him. When he was through, Rachel Wallace signed the bill, added in a tip, and gave it back to him. He smiled—smiled at me—and went out.

Rachel looked at the table. There were flowers in the center.

"You can go for tonight, Spenser," she said. "We'll eat and go to bed. Be here at eight tomorrow."

"Yes, ma'am," I said. "Where we going first?"

"We're going out to Channel Four and do a talk show."

Julie Wells came out of the bathroom. She had a small towel wrapped around her head and a large one wrapped around her body. It covered her but not by much. She said, "Hi, Spenser," and smiled at me. Everyone smiled at me. Lovable. A real pussycat.

"Hello." I didn't belong there. There was something powerfully non-male in the room, and I felt its pressure. "Okay, Rachel. I'll say good night. Don't open the door. Don't even open it to push that cart into the hall. I'll be here at eight."

They both smiled. Neither of them said anything. I went to the door at a normal pace. I did not run. "Don't forget the chain," I said. "And the deadbolt from inside."

They both smiled at me and nodded. Julie Wells's towel seemed to be shrinking. My mouth felt a little dry. "I'll stay outside until I hear the bolt turn."

Smile. Nod.

"Good night," I said, and went out and closed the door. I heard the bolt slide and the chain go in. I went down in the elevator and out onto Arlington Street with my mouth still dry, feeling a bit unlovely.

11

I LEANED AGAINST the cinder-block wall of studio two at Channel Four and watched Rachel Wallace prepare to promote her book and her cause. Off camera a half-dozen technician types in jeans and beards and sneakers hustled about doing technical things.

Rachel sat in a director's chair at a low table. The interviewer was on the other side and on the table between them was a copy of *Tyranny,* standing upright and visible on a small display stand. Rachel sat calmly looking at the camera. The interviewer, a Styrofoam blonde with huge false eyelashes, was smoking a kingsized filter-tipped mentholated Salem cigarette as if they were about to tie her to the post and put on the blindfold. A technician pinned a small microphone to the lapel of Rachel's gray flannel jacket and stepped out of the way. Another technician with a clipboard crouched beneath one of the cameras a foot and a half from the interviewer. He wore earphones.

"Ten seconds, Shirley," he said. The interviewer nodded and snuffed her cigarette out in an ashtray on the floor behind her chair. A man next to me shifted in his folding chair and said, "Jesus Christ, I'm nervous." He was scheduled to talk about raising quail after Rachel had finished. The technician squatting under the front camera pointed at the interviewer.

She smiled. "Hi," she said to the camera. "I'm Shirley. And this is *Contact.* We have with us today feminist and lesbian activist Rachel Wallace. Rachel has written a new book, *Tyranny,* which takes the lid off of some of the ways government and business exploit women and especially gay women. We'll be back to talk with Rachel about her book and these issues after this word." A commercial for hair coloring came on the monitor overhead.

The guy with the earphones crouching beneath the camera said, "Good, Shirl." Shirl took another cigarette from a box on the table behind Rachel's book and lit up. She was able to suck in almost half of it before the guy under the camera said, "Ten seconds." She snuffed this one out, leaned forward slightly, and when the picture came on the monitor, it caught her profile looking seriously at Rachel.

"Rachel," she said, "do you think lesbians ought to be allowed to teach at a girls' school?"

"Quite the largest percentage," Rachel said, "of child molestations are committed by heterosexual men. As I pointed out in my book, the incidence of child molestation by lesbians is so small as to be statistically meaningless."

"But what kind of role model would a lesbian provide?"

"Whatever kind she was. We don't ask other teachers about their sexual habits. We don't prevent so-called frigid women from teaching children, or impotent men. Children do not, it seems to me, have much chance in public school to emulate the sexual habits of their teachers. And if the teacher's sexual preference is so persuasive to his or her students, why aren't gays made straight by exposure to heterosexual teachers?"

"But might not the gay teacher subtly persuade his or her students toward a homosexual preference?"

Rachel said, "I just answered that, Shirley."

Shirley smiled brilliantly. "In your book you allege frequent violations of civil rights in employment both by the government and the private sector. Many of the offenders are here in Massachusetts. Would you care to name some of them?"

Rachel was beginning to look annoyed. "I named all of them in my book," she said.

"But," Shirley said, "not all of our viewers have read it."

"Have you?" Rachel said.

"I haven't finished it yet," Shirley said. "I'm sorry to say." The guy crouching below the camera lens made a gesture with his hand, and Shirley said, "We'll be right back with more interesting revelations from Rachel Wallace after this message."

I whispered to Linda Smith, who stood in neat tweeds beside me, "Shirley doesn't listen to the answers."

"A lot of them don't," Linda said. "They're busy looking ahead to the next question."

"And she hasn't read the book."

Linda smiled and shook her head. "Almost none of them ever do. You can't blame them. Sometimes you get several authors a week plus all the other stuff."

"The pressure must be fearful," I said. "To spend your working life never knowing what you're talking about."

"Lots of people do that," Linda said. "I only hope Rachel doesn't let her annoyance show. She's a good interview, but she gets mad too easy."

"That's because if *she* had been doing the interview, she'd have read the book first."

"Maybe," Linda said, "but Shirley North has a lot of fans in the metropolitan area, and she can sell us some books. The bridge club types love her."

A commercial for pantyhose concluded with a model holding out the crotch to show the ventilated panel, then Shirley came back on.

"In your book, Rachel, you characterize lesbianism as an alternative way of loving. Should everyone try it?"

"Everyone should do what she wants to do," Rachel said. "Obviously people to whom the idea is not attractive should stay straight. My argument is, and has been, that those who do find that alternative desirable should not be victimized for that preference. It does no one any harm at all."

"Is it against God's law?"

"It would be arrogant of me to tell you God's law. I'll leave that to the people who think they have God's ear. All I can say is that I've had no sign that He disapproves."

"How about the argument that it is unnatural?"

"Same answer. That really implies a law of nature that exists immutably. I'm not in a position to know about that. Sartre said that perhaps existence precedes essence, and maybe we are in the process of making the laws of nature as we live."

"Yes, certainly. Do you advocate lesbian marriage?"

"Shirley," Rachel said. "I have documented corruption on several levels of local and state government, in several of the major corporations in the country, and you've asked me only about titillating things. In essence you've asked only about sex. That seems unbalanced to me."

Shirley's smile glowed. Her splendiferous eyelashes fluttered. "Isn't that an interesting thought, Rachel? I wish we could spend more time, but I know you have to rush." She picked up *Tyranny*. "Get Rachel's book, *Tyranny*, published by Hamilton Black. You'll love it, as I did. Thanks a million, Rachel. Come back again."

Rachel muttered, "Thank you."

Shirley said, "Now, this message."

The guy squatting under the camera stood up and said, "Okay, next segment. Thanks a lot Mrs. Wallace. Shirley, you're on the den set." A technician took off Rachel's lapel mike, and she got up and walked away. Shirley didn't say goodbye. She was getting as much mentholated smoke into her as she could before the deodorant commercial ended.

Linda Smith said, "Oh, Rachel, you were dynamite."

Rachel looked at me. I shrugged. Rachel said, "What's that mean?"

I said, "It means you did your best in a difficult situation. You can't look good being interviewed by Shirley North."

Rachel nodded. Linda said, "Oh, no, I thought you were super."

Rachel said nothing as we walked out of the studio and down the long corridor past the news set, empty now and shabby, then along the corridor where people sat in small offices and typed, and out into the lobby and reception area. On the big monitor opposite the reception desk Shirley was leaning toward the man who raised quail.

I frowned the way Shirley did and said in a high voice, "Tell me, do quails like to do it with anything but other quails?"

Rachel gave a snort. Linda smiled. Outside we parted—Rachel and I in my car, Linda in hers.

We wheeled along Soldiers' Field Road with the Charles, quite small and winding this far up, on our left. I looked at Rachel. She was crying. Tears ran in silence down her cheeks. Her hands were folded in her lap. Her shoulders were a little hunched, and her body shook slightly. I looked back at the road. I couldn't think of anything to say. She didn't cry any harder and she didn't stop. The only sound was the unsteady inhaling and exhaling as she cried. We went past Harvard Stadium.

I said, "Feel like a freak?"

She nodded.

"Don't let them do that to you," I said.

"A freak," she said. Her voice was a little thick and a little unsteady, but if you didn't see the tears, you wouldn't be sure she was crying. "Or a monster. That's how everyone seems to see us. Do you seduce little girls? Do you carry them off for strange lesbian rites? Do you use a dildo? God. God damn. Bastards." Her shoulders began to shake harder.

I put my right hand out toward her with the palm up. We passed the business school that way—me with my hand out, her with her body shaking. Then she put her left hand in my right. I held it hard.

"Don't let them do that to you," I said.

She squeezed back at me and we drove the rest of the way along the Charles like that—our hands quite rigidly clamped together, her body slowly quieting down. When I got to the Arlington Street exit, she let go of my hand and opened her purse. By the time we stopped in front of the Ritz, she had her face dry and a little make-up on and herself back in place.

The doorman looked like I'd made a mess on his foot when I got out and nodded toward the Chevy. But he took it from me and said nothing. A job is a job. We went up in the elevator and walked to her room without saying a word. She opened the door. I stepped in first; she followed.

"We have to go to First Mutual Insurance Company at one. I'm addressing a women's group there. Could you pick me up about twelve thirty?" Her voice was quite calm now.

"Sure," I said.

"I'd like to rest for a while," she said, "so please excuse me."

"Sure," I said. "I'll be here at quarter to one."

"Yes," she said. "Thank you."

"Lock the door behind me," I said.

She nodded. I went out and waited until I heard the bolt click behind me. Then I went to the elevator and down.

12

"I'M MEETING WITH a caucus of women employees at First Mutual Insurance," Rachel said. "This is their lunch hour and they've asked me to eat with them. I know you have to be close by, but I would like it if you didn't actually join us." We were walking along Boylston Street.

"Okay," I said. "As I recall from your book, First Mutual is one of the baddies."

"I wouldn't put it that way, but yes. They are discriminatory in their hiring and wage practices. There are almost no women in management. They have systematically refused to employ gay people and have fired any that they discovered in their employ."

"Didn't you turn up discriminatory practices in their sales policy?"

"Yes. They discourage sales to blacks."

"What's the company slogan?"

Rachel smiled. "We're in the people business."

We went into the lobby of First Mutual and took an elevator to the twentieth floor. The cafeteria was at one end of the corridor. A young woman in camel's-hair slacks and vest topped with a dark-brown blazer was waiting outside. When she saw Rachel she came forward and said, "Rachel Wallace?" She wore small gold-rimmed glasses and no make-up. Her hair was brown and sensible.

Rachel put out her hand. "Yes," she said. "Are you Dorothy Collela?"

"Yes, come on in. We're all at a table in the corner." She looked at me uncertainly.

"My name is Spenser," I said. "I just hang around Ms. Wallace. Don't think about me for a moment."

"Will you be joining us?" Dorothy said.

Rachel said, "No. Mr. Spenser is just going to stay by if I need anything."

Dorothy smiled a little blankly and led Rachel to a long table at one end of the cafeteria. There were eight other women gathered there. I leaned against the wall maybe twenty feet away where I could see Rachel and not hear them and not be in the flow of diners.

There was a good deal of chair-scraping and jostling at the table when Rachel sat down. There were introductions and people standing and sitting, and then all but two of the women got up and went to the food line to get lunch. The luncheon special was Scrambled Hamburg Oriental, and I decided to pass on lunch.

The cafeteria had a low ceiling with a lot of fluorescent panels in it. The walls were painted a brilliant yellow on three sides with a bank of windows looking out over Back

Bay on the fourth side. The bright yellow paint was almost painful. Music filtered through the cafeteria noise. It sounded like Mantovani, but it always does.

Working with a writer, you get into the glamour scene. After we left here, we'd probably go down to Filene's basement and autograph corsets. Maybe Norman would be there, and Truman and Gore. Rachel took her tray and sat down. She had eschewed the Oriental hamburg. On her tray was a sandwich and a cup of tea.

A girl not long out of the high-school corridors came past me wearing very expensive clothes, very snugly. She had on blue harlequin glasses with small jewels on them, and she smelled like a French sunset.

She smiled at me and said, "Well, foxy, what are you looking at?"

"A size-nine body in a size-seven dress," I said.

"You should see it without the dress," she said.

"I certainly should," I said.

She smiled and joined two other kids her age at a table. They whispered together and looked at me and laughed. The best-dressed people in the world are the single kids that just started working.

Two men in business suits and one uniformed guard came into the cafeteria and walked over to Rachel's table. I slid along behind and listened in. It looked like my business. It was.

"We invited her here," Dorothy was saying.

One of the business suits said, "You're not authorized to do that." He looked like Clark Kent. Three-piece suit with a small gray herringbone in it. Glasses, square face. His hair was short, his face was clean shaved. His shoes were shined. His tie was knotted small but asserted by a simple pin. He was on the way up.

"Who are you?" Rachel said.

"Timmons," he said. "Director of employee relations." He spoke very fast. "This is Mr. Boucher, our security coordinator." Nobody introduced the uniformed guard; he wasn't on the way up. Boucher was sort of plumpish and had a thick mustache. The guard didn't have a gun, but the loop of a leather strap stuck out of his right hip pocket.

"And why are you asking me to leave?" Rachel was saying.

"Because you are in violation of company policy."

"How so?"

"No soliciting is allowed on the premises," Timmons said. I wondered if he was nervous or if he always spoke that fast. I drifted around behind Rachel's chair and folded my arms and looked at Timmons.

"And what exactly am I supposed to be soliciting?" Rachel said.

Timmons didn't like me standing there, and he didn't quite know what to do about it. He looked at me and looked away quickly and then he looked at Boucher and back at me and then at Rachel. He started to speak to Rachel and stopped and looked at me again.

"Who are you?" he said.

"I'm the tooth fairy," I said.

"The what?"

"The tooth fairy," I said. "I loosen teeth."

Timmons's mouth opened and shut. Boucher said, "We don't need any smart answers, mister."

I said, "You wouldn't understand any."

Rachel said, "Mr. Spenser is with me."

"Well," Boucher said, "you'll both have to leave or we'll have you removed."

"How many security people you got?" I said to Boucher.

"That's no concern of yours," Boucher said. Very tough.

"Yeah, but it could be a concern of yours. It will take an awful lot of people like you to remove us."

The uniformed guard looked uncomfortable. He probably knew his limitations, or maybe he just didn't like the company he was keeping.

"Spenser," Rachel said, "I don't want any of that. We will resist, but we will resist passively."

The dining room was very quiet except for the yellow walls. Timmons spoke again—probably encouraged by the mention of passive resistance.

"Will you leave quietly?" he said.

"No," Rachel said, "I will not."

"Then you leave us no choice," Boucher said. He turned to the uniformed guard. "Spag," he said, "take her out."

"You can't do that," Dorothy said.

"You should wait and discuss this with your supervisor," Timmons said, "because I certainly will."

Spag stepped forward and said softly, "Come on, miss."

Rachel didn't move.

Boucher said, "Take her, Spag."

Spag took her arm, gently. "Come on, miss, you gotta go," he said. He kept a check on me with frequent side-shifting glances. He was probably fifty and no more than 170 pounds, some of it waistline. He had receding brown hair and tattoos on both forearms. He pulled lightly at Rachel's arm. She went limp.

Boucher said, "God damn it, Spag, yank her out of that chair. She's trespassing. You have the right."

Spag let go of Rachel's arm and straightened up. "No," he said. "I guess not."

Timmons said, "Jesus Christ."

Boucher said to him, "All right, we'll do it. Brett, you take one arm." He stepped forward and took Rachel under the left arm. Timmons took her right arm, and they dragged her out of the chair. She went limp on them, and they weren't ready for it. They couldn't hold her dead weight, and she slipped to the floor, her legs spread, her skirt hitched halfway up her thigh. She pulled it down.

I said to Spag, "I am going to make a move here. Are you in or out?"

Spag looked at Rachel on the floor and at Timmons and Boucher. "Out," he said. "I used to do honest work."

Boucher was behind Rachel now and had both his arms under hers. I said to him, "Let her go."

Rachel said, "Spenser, I told you we were going to be passive."

Boucher said, "You stay out of this, or you'll be in serious trouble."

I said, "Let go of her, or I'll hit you while you're bent over."

Timmons said, "Hey," but it wasn't loud.

Boucher let Rachel go and stood up. Everyone in the dining room was standing and watching. There was a lot on the line for Boucher. I felt sorry for him. Most of the onlookers were young women. I reached my hand down to Rachel. She took it and got up.

"God damn you," she said. I turned toward her and

Boucher took a jump at me. He wasn't big, but he was slow. I dropped my shoulder and caught him in the chest. He grunted. I straightened up, and he staggered backwards and bumped into Timmons.

I said, "If you annoy me, I will knock you right over that serving counter." I pointed my finger at him.

Rachel said, "You stupid bastard," and slapped me across the face. Boucher made another jump. I hit him a stiff jab in the nose and then crossed with my right, and he went back into the serving line and knocked down maybe fifty plates off the counter and slid down to the floor. "Into is almost as good as over," I said. Timmons was stuck. He had to do something. He took a swing at me; I pulled my head back, slapped his arm on past me with my right hand. It half turned him. I got his collar in my left hand and the seat of his pants in my right and ran him three steps over to the serving counter, braced my feet, arched my back a little, and heaved him up and over it. One of his arms went in the gravy. Mashed potatoes smeared his chest, and he went over the counter rolling and landed on his side on the floor behind it.

The young girl with the tight clothes said, "All *right,* foxy," and started to clap. Most of the women in the cafeteria joined in. I went back to Rachel. "Come on," I said. "Someone must have called the cops. We'd best walk out with dignity. Don't slap me again till we're outside."

13

"YOU DUMB son of a bitch," Rachel said. We were walking along Boylston Street back to the Ritz. "Don't you realize that it would have been infinitely more productive to allow them to drag me out in full view of all those women?"

"Productive of what?"

"Of an elevated consciousness on the part of all those women who were standing there watching the management of that company dramatize its sexism."

"What kind of a bodyguard stands around and lets two B-school twerps like those drag out the body he's supposed to be guarding?"

"An intelligent one. One who understands his job. You're employed to keep me alive, not to exercise your Arthurian fantasies." We turned left on Arlington. Across the street a short gray-haired man wearing two topcoats vomited on the base of the statue of William Ellery Channing.

"Back there you embodied everything I hate," Rachel said. "Everything I have tried to prevent. Everything I have denounced—machismo, violence, that preening male arrogance that compels a man to defend any woman he's with, regardless of her wishes and regardless of her need."

"Don't beat around the bush," I said. "Come right out and say you disapprove of my conduct."

"It demeaned me. It assumed I was helpless and dependent, and needed a big strong man to look out for me. It reiterated that image to all those young women who broke into mindless applause when it was over."

We were in front of the Ritz. The doorman smiled at us—probably pleased that I didn't have my car.

"Maybe that's so," I said. "Or maybe that's a lot of theory which has little to do with practice. I don't care very much about theory or the long-range consequences to the class struggle, or whatever. I can't deal with that. I work close up. Right then I couldn't let them drag you out while I stood around."

"Of course from your viewpoint you'd be dishonored. I'm just the occasion for your behavior, not the reason. The reason is pride—you didn't do that for me, and don't try to kid yourself."

The doorman's smile was getting a little forced.

"I'd do it again," I said.

"I'm sure you would," Rachel said, "but you'll have to do it with someone else. You and I are terminated. I don't want you around me. Whatever your motives, they are not mine, and I'll not violate my life's convictions just to keep your pride intact."

She turned and walked into the Ritz. I looked at the

doorman. He was looking at the Public Garden. "The hell of it is," I said to him, "I think she was probably right."

"That makes it much worse," he said.

I walked back along Arlington and back up Boylston for a block to Berkeley Street. I had several choices. I could go down to the Dockside Saloon and drink all their beer, or I could drive up to Smithfield and wait till Susan came home from school and tell her I flunked Women's Lib. Or I could do something useful. I opted for useful and turned up Berkeley.

Boston Police Headquarters was a block and a half up Berkeley Street on the right, nestled in the shadows of big insurance companies—probably made the cops feel safe. Martin Quirk's office at the end of the Homicide squadroom was just as it always was. The room was neat and spare. The only thing on the desk was a phone and a plastic cube with pictures of his family in it.

Quirk was on the phone when I appeared in his doorway. He was tilted back in his chair, his feet on the desk, the phone hunched against his ear with his shoulder. He pointed at the straight chair beside his desk, and I sat down.

"Physical evidence," Quirk said into the phone. "What have you got for physical evidence?" He listened. His tweed jacket hung on the back of his chair. His white shirt was crisp and starchy. The cuffs were turned under once over his thick wrists. He was wearing over the ankle cordovan shoes with brass buckles. The shoes shined with fresh polish. The gray slacks were sharply creased. The black knit tie was knotted and in place. His thick black hair was cut short with no sign of gray.

"Yeah, I know," he said into the phone. "But we got no choice. Get it." He hung up and looked at me. "Don't you ever wear a tie?" he said.

"Just the other day," I said. "Dinner at the Ritz."

"Well you ought to do it more often. You look like a goddamned overage hippie."

"You're jealous of my youthful image," I said. "Just because you're a bureaucrat and have to dress up like Calvin Coolidge doesn't mean I have to. It's the difference between you and me."

"There's other differences," Quirk said. "What do you want?"

"I want to know what you know about threats on the life of Rachel Wallace."

"Why?"

"Until about a half hour ago I was her bodyguard."

"And?"

"And she fired me for being too masculine."

"Better than the other way around, I guess," Quirk said.

"But I figured since I'd been hired by the day I might as well use the rest of it to see what I could find out from you."

"There isn't much to tell. She reported the threats. We looked into it. Nothing much surfaced. I had Belson ask around on the street. Nobody knew anything."

"You have any opinion on how serious the threats are?"

Quirk shrugged. "If I had to guess, I'd guess they could be. Belson couldn't find any professional involvement. She names a lot of names and makes a lot of embarrassing charges about local businesses and government figures, but that's all they are—embarrassing. Nobody's going to go to jail or end his career, or whatever."

"Which means," I said, "if the threats are real, they are probably from some coconut, or group of coconuts, that are anti-feminist or anti-gay, or both."

"That would be my guess," Quirk said. "The busing issue in this town has solidified and organized all the redneck crazies. So any radical issue comes along, there's half a dozen little fringe outfits available to oppose it. A lot of them don't have anything to do now that busing is getting to be routine. For crissake they took the state cops out of South Boston High this year."

"Educational reform," I said. "One comes to expect such innovation in the Athens of America."

Quirk grunted and locked his hands behind his head as he leaned back further in his chair. The muscles in his upper arm swelled against the shirt sleeve.

"So who's looking after her now?" he said.

"Nobody that I know of. That's why I'm interested in the reality of the threats."

"You know how it is," Quirk said. "We got no facts. How can we? Anonymous phonecalls don't lead anywhere. If I had to guess, I guess there might be some real danger."

"Yeah, me too," I said. "What bothers you?"

"Well, the threat to harm her if the book wasn't suppressed. I mean, there were already copies of the damned thing around in galleys or whatever they are. The damage had been done."

"Why doesn't that make you feel easier?" I said. "Why isn't it just a crank call, or a series of crank calls?"

"How would a crank caller even know about the book? Or her? I'm not saying it's sure. I mean it could be some numb-nuts in the publishing company, or at the printer, or anywhere that they might see the book. But it feels worse than that. It has a nice, steady hostile feel of organized opposition."

"Balls," I said.

"You don't agree," Quirk said.

"No. I do. That's what bothers me. It feels real to me, too. Like people who want that book suppressed not because it tells secrets, but because it argues something they don't want to hear."

Quirk nodded. "Right. It's not a matter of keeping a secret. If we're right, and we're both guessing, it's opposition to her opinion and her expression of it. But we are both guessing."

"Yeah, but we're good guessers," I said. "We have some experience in the field."

Quirk shrugged. "We'll see," he said.

"Also, somebody made what looked like a professional try at her a couple nights ago."

"Good how promptly you reported it to the authorities," Quirk said.

"I'm doing that now," I said. "Listen."

He listened.

I told him about the two-car incident on the Lynnway. I told him about the pickets in Belmont and the pie-throwers in Cambridge. I told him about the recent unpleasantness in the First Mutual cafeteria.

"Don't you freelance types have an exciting time of it?" Quirk said.

"It makes the time pass," I said.

"The business on the Lynnway is the only thing that sounds serious," Quirk said. "Gimme the license numbers."

I did.

"Course they could be merely harassing you like the others."

"They seemed to know their way around."

"Shit, everybody knows his way around. They watch *Baretta* and *Kojak*. They know all about that stuff."

"Yeah," I said. "Could be. Could even be a pattern."

"Conspiracy?" Quirk raised both eyebrows.

"Possible."

"But likely?"

I shrugged. "There are stranger things in this world than in all your philosophies, Horatio."

"The only other guy I ever met as intellectual as you," Quirk said, "was a child molester we put away in the late summer of 1967."

"Smart doesn't mean good," I said.

"I've noted that," Quirk said. "Anyway, I'm not ready to buy a conspiracy without more."

"Me either," I said. "Can you do anything about keeping an eye on her?"

"I'll call Callahan over at the Ritz again. Tell him you're off the thing, and he should be a little carefuller."

"That's it?"

"Yeah," Quirk said, "that's it. I need more people than I've got now. I can't put a guard on her. If she makes a public appearance somewhere, maybe I can arrange to beef up her security a little. But we both know the score—I can't protect her and neither can you, unless she wants us to. And even then"—he shrugged—"depends on how bad somebody wants her."

"But after someone does her in, you'll swing into action. Then you'll be able to spare a dozen men."

"Take a walk," Quirk said. The lines from his nose to

the corners of his mouth were deep. "I don't need to get lectured about police work. I'm still here—I didn't quit."

I stood up. "I apologize," I said. "I feel very sour about things now. I'm blaming you."

Quirk nodded. "I get anything on those numbers, you want to know?"

"Yeah."

"Okay."

I left.

14

SUSAN AND I were at the raw bar in the middle of Quincy Market eating oysters and drinking beer, and arguing. Sort of.

"So why didn't you keep out of it?" Susan said. "Rachel had asked you to."

"And stand there and let them drag her out?"

"Yes." Susan slurped an oyster off the shell. They don't offer forks at the raw bar. They just serve oysters or clams or shrimp, with beer in paper cups. There are bowls of oyster crackers and squeeze bottles of cocktail sauce. They named the place the Walrus and the Carpenter, but I like it anyway.

"I couldn't do that," I said. Under the vaulted ceiling of the market, people swirled up and down the main aisle. A bearded man wearing a ski cap and a green turtleneck sweater eyed Susan and whispered something to the man with him. The man with him looked at Susan and nodded.

They both smiled, and then they both caught me looking at them and looked away and moved on. I ordered another beer. Susan sipped a little of hers.

"Why couldn't you do that?" Susan said.

"It violates something."

"What?"

I shrugged. "My pride?"

Susan nodded. "Now we're getting somewhere. And while we're at it, if somebody wants to admire my figure, why not let them? I am pleased. Would it be better if they didn't?"

"You mean those two clowns a minute ago?"

"Yes. And a man who admires my ass isn't necessarily a clown."

"I didn't do anything," I said.

"You glared at them."

"Well, they scare easy."

"Would you have liked it better if they'd told me to start wearing a girdle?"

I said, "Grrrrr."

"Exactly. So what are you glaring at them for?"

"My pride?"

"Now we're getting somewhere."

"Didn't we just have this conversation?"

She smiled and gestured at the bartender for another beer. "Yes, but we haven't finished it."

"So what should I have done when those two upwardly mobile assholes took hold of her?"

"Stood by, made sure they didn't hurt her. Been available if she called for help. Held the door as they went out."

"Jesus Christ," I said.

"Or you could have locked arms with her and gone limp when they touched you and made it that much harder."

"No," I said. "I couldn't do that. Maybe I could have stood by, or maybe if there were a next time I could. But I couldn't lie down and let them drag me out."

"No. You couldn't. But you didn't have to deprive Rachel of a chance for a triumph."

"I didn't think of it in just that way."

"Of course you didn't—just as you don't perceive it that way when we're at a party and someone makes a pass at me and you're at his shoulder with the look."

"Depriving you of the chance to deal with it successfully yourself."

"Of course," she said. There was a small streak of cocktail sauce at one corner of her mouth. I reached over and wiped it away with my thumb. "I don't normally need you to protect me. I got along quite well without you for quite some years. I fended off the people I wanted to fend off, all by myself."

"And if they don't fend?"

"I call you. You're not far. I've not seen you ten feet from me at a party since we met."

I finished my beer. "Let's walk up toward the Faneuil Hall end," I said. It was nearly four thirty and the crowds were thin, for the market. "Maybe I'll buy you a croissant."

"I'm not bitching about me," she said. She put her arm through mine. Her head came a little above my shoulder. Her hair had a faint flowery smell. "I understand you, and I kind of like your proprietary impulses. Also I love you, and it changes one's perspective sometimes."

"We could slip into that stairwell and make out," I said.

"Later. You promised a lot of walking and eating and drinking and looking at people."

"And after that?"

"Who knows?" Susan said. "Maybe ecstasy."

"Let's walk faster then."

Quincy Market is old and lovingly restored. It is vast and made of granite blocks. Along each side of the long center aisle there were stalls selling yogurt with fruit topping, kielbasy on a roll with sauerkraut, lobster rolls, submarine sandwiches, French bread, country pâté, Greek salad, sweet and sour chicken, baklava, cookies, bagels, oysters, cheese, fresh fruit on a stick, ice cream, cheesecake, barbecued chicken, pizza, doughnuts, cookies, galantine of duck, roast beef sandwiches with chutney on fresh-baked bread, bean sprouts, dried peaches, jumbo cashews and other nuts. There are also butchershops, cheese stores, a place that sells custom-ground coffee, fruit stands, and a place that sells Korean ginseng root. Outside on either side are arcades with more stalls and terrace cafés, and in restored brick buildings parallel were clothing stores and specialty shops and restaurants. It claims to be the number-one tourist attraction in Boston, and it should be. If you were with a girl in the market area, it would be hard not to hold hands with her. Jugglers and strolling musicians moved around the area. The market is never empty, and in prime time it is nearly unmanageable. We stopped and bought two skewers of fresh fruit and melon, and ate them as we walked.

"What you say makes sense, babe," I said, "but it doesn't feel right."

"I know," she said. "It probably never will for you. You were brought up with a fierce sense of family. But you haven't got a family, and so you transfer that great sea of protective impulse to clients, and me."

"Maybe not you, but usually clients need protection."

"Yes. That's probably why you're in business. You need people who need protection. Otherwise what would you do with the impulse?"

I threw my empty skewer in a trash barrel. "Concentrate it all on you, chickie," I said.

Susan said, "Oh, God."

"I don't think I'm going to change," I said.

"Oh, I hope you don't. I love you. And I understand you, and you should stay as sweet as you are. But you can see why Rachel Wallace might have reservations about you."

"Yeah, except I'm so goddamned cute," I said.

"You certainly are that," Susan said. "Want to split a yogurt?"

15

IT WAS THREE weeks before Christmas, and it was snowing big sporadic flakes outside my office window when I found out that they'd taken Rachel Wallace.

I was sitting with my feet up, drinking black coffee and eating a doughnut and waiting for a guy named Anthony Gonsalves to call me from Fall River when the phone rang. It wasn't Gonsalves.

A voice said, "Spenser? John Ticknor from Hamilton Black. Could you get over here right now? It appears Rachel Wallace has been kidnaped."

"Did you call the cops?" I said.

"Yes."

"Okay, I'm on my way."

I hung up, put my fleece-lined jacket on over my black turtleneck and shoulder holster, and went. My office that year was on the corner of Mass. Ave. and Boylston Street, on the second floor, in a small three-sided turret over a smokeshop. My car was parked by a sign that said No Parking Bus Stop. I got in and drove straight down Boylston. The snow was melting as it hit the street but collecting on the margins of the road and on the sidewalks and building ledges.

The Christmas tree in the Prudential Center was lit already although it was only three forty-five. I turned left at Charles and right onto Beacon and parked at the top of the hill in front of the State House in a space that said Reserved for Members of the General Court. They meant the legislature, but Massachusetts calls it the Great and General Court for the same reason they call themselves a Commonwealth. It has something to do I think with not voting for Nixon. To my right the Common sloped down to Tremont Street, its trees strung with Christmas lights, a very big Nativity scene stretching out near the Park Street end. The snow was holding on the grass part of the Common and melting on the walkways. Down near the information booth they had some reindeer in pens, and a guy with a sandwich board was standing by the pens handing leaflets to people who were trying to feed popcorn to the deer.

Ticknor's office was on the top floor looking out over the Common. It was high-ceilinged and big-windowed and cluttered with books and manuscripts. Across from the desk was a low couch, and in front of the couch was a coffee table covered with manila folders. Ticknor was sitting on the couch with his feet on the coffee table looking out at the guy on the Common who was handing out leaflets by the reindeer pens. Frank Belson, who was a detective-sergeant, sat on the couch beside him and sipped some coffee. A young guy with a face from County Mayo and a three-piece suit from Louis was standing behind Ticknor's desk talking on the phone.

Belson nodded at me as I came in. I looked at the kid with the County Mayo face and said, "DA's office?"

Belson nodded. "Cronin," he said. "Assistant prosecutor."

Ticknor said, "Spenser, I'm glad you could come. You know Sergeant Belson, I gather."

I nodded.

Ticknor said, "This is Roger Forbes, our attorney."

I shook hands with a tall gray-haired man with high cheekbones and sunken cheeks who stood—a little uncomfortably, I thought—in the corner between the couch and a book shelf.

Cronin said into the phone, "We haven't said anything to the media yet."

I said to Belson, "What have you got?"

He handed me a typewritten sheet of paper. It was neatly typed, double-spaced. No strikeovers, no x-ed out portions. Margins were good. Paragraphs were indented five spaces. It was on a plain sheet of Eaton's Corrasable Bond. It read:

> Whereas Rachel Wallace has written several books offensive to God and country; whereas she has advocated lesbian love in direct contradiction of the Bible and common decency; whereas she has corrupted and continues to corrupt our nation and our children through the public media, which mindlessly exploits her for greed; and whereas our public officials, content to be the dupes of any radical conspiracy, have taken no action, therefore we have been forced to move.

We have taken her and are holding her. She has not been harmed, and unless you fail to follow our instructions, she will not be. We want no money. We have taken action in the face of a moral imperative higher than any written law, and we shall follow that imperative though it lead to the grave.

Remain alert for further communication. We will submit our demands to you for communication to the appropriate figures. Our demands are not negotiable. If they are not met, the world will be better for the death of Rachel Wallace.

R(estore) A(merican) M(orality)
RAM

I read it twice. It said the same thing both times. "Some prose style," I said to Ticknor.

"If you'd been able to get along with her," Ticknor said, "perhaps the note would never have been written." His face was a little flushed.

I said to Belson, "And you've checked it out."

"Sure," Belson said. "She's nowhere. Her hotel room is empty. Suitcases are still there, stuff still in drawers. She was supposed to be on a radio talk show this afternoon and never showed. Last time anyone saw her was last night around nine o'clock, when the room service waiter brought up some sandwiches and a bottle of gin and one of vermouth and two glasses. He says there was someone taking a shower, but he doesn't know who. The bathroom door was closed, and he heard the water running."

"And you got nothing for a lead."

"Not a thing," Belson said. He was lean and thin-faced with a beard so heavy that the lower half of his face had a blue cast to it, even though he shaved at least twice a day. He smoked five-cent cigars down to the point where the live end burned his lip, and he had one going now that was only halfway there but already chewed and battered-looking.

"Quirk coming in on this," I said.

"Yeah, he'll be along in a while. He had to be in court this afternoon, and he sent me down to get started. But now that you showed up, he probably won't need to."

Cronin hung up the phone and looked at me. "Who are you?"

Ticknor said, "Mr. Spenser was hired to protect her. We thought he might be able to shed some light on the situation."

"Sure did a hell of a job protecting," Cronin said. "You know anything?"

"Not much," I said.

"Didn't figure you would. They want you around, okay by me, but don't get in the way. You annoy me, and I'll roast your ass."

I looked at Belson. He grinned. "They're turning them out tougher and tougher up the heights," Belson said.

"This must be their supreme achievement," I said. "They'll never get one tougher than this."

"Knock off the shit," Cronin said. "Sergeant, you know this guy?"

"Oh, yes, sir, Mr. Cronin. I know him. You want me to shoot him?"

"What the hell is wrong with you, Belson? I asked you a simple question."

"He's all right," Belson said. "He'll be a help."

"He better be," Cronin said. "Spenser, I want you to give Sergeant Belson a rundown on anything you know about this case. Belson, if there's anything worth it, get a formal statement."

"Yeah, sure," Belson said. "Get right on it." He winked at me.

Cronin turned to Ticknor. "You're in the word business. You recognize anything from the way it's written, the prose style?"

"If it were a manuscript, we'd reject it," Ticknor said. "Other than that I haven't anything to say about it. I can't possibly guess who wrote it."

Cronin wasn't really listening. He turned toward Forbes, the lawyer. "Is there a room around here where we can meet with the media people, Counselor?" He addressed Forbes almost like an equal; law-school training probably gave him an edge.

"Certainly," Forbes said. "We've a nice conference room on the second floor that will do, I think." He spoke to Ticknor. "I'll take him to the Hamilton Room, John."

"Good idea," Ticknor said. Forbes led the way out. Cronin stopped at the door. "I want everything this guy knows, Sergeant. I want him empty when he leaves."

I said to Belson, "I don't want my face marked up."

"Who could tell?" he said.

Cronin went out after Forbes.

I sat on the edge of Ticknor's desk. "I hope he doesn't go armed," I said.

"Cronin?" Belson laughed. "He got out of law school in 1973, the year I first took the lieutenant's exam. He thinks if he's rough and tough, people won't notice that he doesn't know shit and just wants to get elected to public office."

"He figures wrong," Ticknor said. Belson raised his eyebrows approvingly. Ticknor was behind him and didn't see.

I said to Ticknor, "How'd you get the letter?"

"Someone delivered it to the guard at the desk downstairs," Ticknor said. He handed me the envelope. It was blank except for Ticknor's name typed on the front.

"Description?"

Belson answered. "They get a hundred things a day delivered down there. Guard paid no attention. Can't remember for sure even whether it was a man or a woman."

"It's not his fault," Ticknor said. "We get all sorts of deliveries from the printers—galleys, pages, blues—as well as manuscripts from agents, authors, and readers, artwork, and half a dozen other kinds of material at the desk every day. Walt isn't expected to pay attention to who brings it."

I nodded. "Doesn't matter. Probably someone hired a cabby to bring it in anyway, and descriptions don't help much, even if they're good ones."

Belson nodded. "I already got somebody checking the cab companies for people who had things delivered here. But they could just as easy have delivered it themselves."

"Should the press be in on this?" Ticknor said.

"I don't think it does much harm," I said. "And I don't think you could keep them out of here if Cronin has any say. This sounds like an organization that wants publicity. They said nothing about keeping it from the press, just as they said nothing about keeping the police out."

"I agree," Belson said. "Most kidnapings have something about 'don't go to the police,' but these political or social or whatever-the-hell-they-are kidnapings usually are after publicity. And anyway Cronin has already told the press so the question is—what? What word am I after?"

Ticknor said, "Academic. Hypothetical. Aimless. Too late. Merely conjectural."

"Okay, any of those," Belson said.

"So what do we do?" Ticknor said.

"Nothing much," Belson said. "We sit. We wait. Some of us ask around on the street. We check with the FBI to see if they have anything on RAM. We have the paper analyzed and the ink, and learn nothing from either. In a while somebody will get in touch and tell us what they want."

"That's all?" Ticknor was offended. He looked at me.

"I don't like it either," I said. "But that's about all. Mostly we have to wait for contact. The more contact the better. The more in touch they are, the more we have to work on, the better chance we have to find them. And her."

"But how can we be sure they'll make contact?"

Belson answered. "You can't. But you figure they will. They said they would. They did this for a reason. They want something. One of the things you can count on is that everybody wants something." The cigar had burned down far enough now so that Belson had to tilt his head slightly to keep the smoke from getting in his eyes.

"But in the meantime—what about Rachel? My God, think how she must feel. Suppose they abuse her? We can't just sit here and wait."

Belson looked at me. I said, "We haven't got anything else to do. There's no profit in thinking about alternatives when you don't have any. She's a tough woman. She'll do as well as anyone."

"But alone," Ticknor said, "with these maniacs. . . ."

"Think about something else," Belson said. "Have you any idea who this group might be?"

Ticknor shook his head briskly, as if he had a fly in his ear. "No," he said. "No. No idea at all. What do they call themselves? RAM?"

Belson nodded. "Anyone in the publishing community that you know of that has any hostility toward Ms. Wallace?"

"No, well, I mean, not like this. Rachel is abrasive and difficult, and she advocates things not everyone likes, but nothing that would cause a kidnaping."

"Let us decide that. You just give me a list of everybody you can think of that didn't like her, that argued with her, that disagreed with her."

"My God, man, that would include half the reviewers in the country."

"Take your time," Belson said. He had a notebook out and leaned back in his chair.

"But, my God, Sergeant, I can't just start listing names indiscriminately. I mean, I'll be involving these people in the investigation of a capital crime."

"Aren't you the one was worried about how poor Rachel must be feeling?" Belson said.

I knew the conversation. I'd heard variations on it too many times. I said, "I'm going to go out and look for Rachel. Let me know when you hear from them."

"I'm not authorized to employ you on this, Spenser," Ticknor said.

Belson said, "Me either." His thin face had the look of internal laughter.

"All part of the service," I said.

I went out of Ticknor's office, past two detectives questioning a secretary, into the elevator down to the street, and out to start looking.

16

THE BOSTON *Globe* is in a building on Morrissey Boulevard which looks like the offspring of a warehouse and a suburban junior high school. It used to be on Washington Street in the middle of the city and looked like a newspaper building should. But that was back when the *Post* was still with us, and the *Daily Record.* Only yesterday. When the world was young.

It was the day after they took Rachel and snowing again. I was talking to Wayne Cosgrove in the city room about right-wing politics, on which he'd done a series three years earlier.

"I never heard of RAM," he said. Cosgrove was thirty-five, with a blond beard. He had on wide-wale corduroy pants and a gray woolen shirt and a brown tweed jacket. His feet were up on the desk. On them he wore leather boots with rubber bottoms and yellow laces. A blue down parka with a hood hung on the back of his chair.

"God you look slick, Wayne," I said. "You must have been a Nieman Fellow some time."

"A year at Harvard," he said, "picks up your taste like a bastard." He'd grown up in Newport News, Virginia, and still had the sound of it when he talked.

"I can see that," I said. "Why don't you look in your files and see if you have anything on RAM?"

"Files," Cosgrove said, "I don't need to show no stinking files, gringo." He told me once that he'd seen *The Treasure of the Sierra Madre* four times at a revival house in Cambridge.

"You don't have any files?"

He shrugged. "Some, but the good stuff is up here, in the old coconut. And there ain't nothing on RAM. Doesn't matter. Groups start up and fold all the time, like sub sandwich shops. Or they change the name, or a group splinters off from another one. If I had done that series day before yesterday, I might not have heard of RAM, and they might be this week's biggie. When I did the series, most of the dippos were focused on busing. All the mackerel-snappers were afraid of the niggers' fucking their daughters, and the only thing they could think of to prevent that was to keep the niggers away from their daughters. Don't seem to speak too highly of their daughters' self-control, but anyway if you wanted to get a group started, then you went over to Southie and yelled *nigger nigger.*"

He pronounced it *niggah.*

"Isn't that a technique that was developed regionally?"

"Ahhh, yes," Cosgrove said. "Folks down home used to campaign for office on that issue, whilst you folks up north was just a tsk-tsking at us and sending in the feds. Fearful racism there was, in the South, in those days."

"Didn't I hear you were involved in freedom riding, voter registration, and Communist subversion in Mississippi some years back?"

"I had a northern granddaddy," Cosgrove said. "Musta come through on a gene."

"So where are all the people in this town who used to stand around chanting *never* and throwing rocks at children?"

Cosgrove said, "Most of them are saying, 'Well, hardly ever.' But I know what you're after. Yeah, I'd say some of them, having found out that a lot of the niggers don't want to fuck their daughters, are now sweating that the faggots will bugger their sons and are getting up a group to throw rocks at fairies."

"Any special candidates?"

Cosgrove shrugged, "Aw, shit, I don't know, buddy. You know as well as I do that the hub of any ultra-right-wing piece of business in this metropolitan area is Fix Farrell. For Christ's sake, he's probably anti-Eskimo."

"Yeah, I know about Farrell, but I figure a guy like him wouldn't involve himseif in a thing like this."

" 'Cause he's on the city council?" Cosgrove said. "How the hell old are you?"

"I don't argue he's honest, I just argue he doesn't need this kind of action. I figure a guy like him benefits from people like Rachel Wallace. Gives him someone to be against. Farrell wouldn't want her kidnaped and her book suppressed. He'd want her around selling it at the top of her lungs so he could denounce her and promulgate plans to thwart her."

Cosgrove tapped his teeth with the eraser end of a yellow

pencil. "Not bad," he said. "You probably got a pretty good picture of Fix at that."

"You think he might have any thoughts on who I should look into?"

Cosgrove shook his head very quickly. "No soap. Farrell's never going to rat on a possible vote—and anybody opposed to a gay feminist activist can't be all bad in Fix's book."

"You think the RAM people would trust him?" I said.

"How the fuck would I know?" Cosgrove said. "Jesus, Spenser, you are a plugger, I'll say that for you."

"Hell of a bodyguard, too," I said.

Cosgrove shrugged. "I'll ask around; I'll talk it up in the city room. I hear anything, I'll give you a buzz."

"Thank you," I said, and left.

17

I KNEW A guy who was in the Ku Klux Klan. His name was Manfred Roy, and I had helped bust him once, when I was on the cops, for possession of pornographic materials. It was a while ago, when possession of pornographic materials was more serious business than it is now. And Manfred had weaseled on the guy he bought it from and the friends who were with him when he bought it, and we dropped the charges against him and his name never got in the papers. He lived with his mother, and she would have been disappointed in him if she had known. After I left the cops, I kept track of Manfred. How many people do you know that actually belong to the Ku Klux Klan? You find one, you don't lose him.

Manfred was working that year cutting hair in a barbershop on the ground floor of the Park Square Building. He was a small guy, with white-blond hair in a crew cut. Under his barber coat he had on a plaid flannel shirt and chino pants and brown penny-loafers with a high shine. It wasn't a trendy shop. The only razor cut you got was if somebody nicked you while they were shaving your neck.

I sat in the waiting chair and read the *Globe*. There was an article on the city council debate over a bond issue. I read the first paragraph because Wayne Cosgrove had a byline, but even loyalty flagged by paragraph two.

There were four barbers working. One of them, a fat guy with an Elvis Presley pompadour sprayed into rigid stillness, said, "Next?"

I said, "No thanks. I'll wait for him," and pointed at Manfred.

He was cutting the hair of a white-haired man. He glanced toward me and then back at the man and then realized who I was and peeked at me in the mirror. I winked at him, and he jerked his eyes back down at the white hair in front of him.

In five minutes he finished up with Whitey and it was my turn. I stepped to the chair. Manfred said, "I'm sorry, sir, it's my lunch hour, perhaps another barber. . . ?"

I gave him a big smile and put my arm around him. "That's even better, Manfred. Actually I just wanted to have a good rap with you anyway. I'll buy you lunch."

"Well, actually, I was meeting somebody."

"Swell, I'll rap with them, too. Come on, Manfred. Long time no see."

The barber with the pompadour was looking at us. Manfred slipped off his white barber coat, and we went together out the door of the shop. I took my coat from the rack as I went by.

In the corridor outside Manfred said, "God damn you, Spenser, you want to get me fired?"

"Manfred," I said, "Manfred. How unkind. Un-Christian even. I came by to see you and buy you lunch."

"Why don't you just leave me alone?" he said.

"You still got any of those inflatable rubber nude girls you used to be dealing?"

We were walking along the arcade in the Park Square Building. The place had once been stylish and then gotten very unstylish and was now in renaissance. Manfred was looking at his feet as we walked.

"I was different then," Manfred said. "I had not found Christ yet."

"You, too?" I said.

"I wouldn't expect you to understand."

Near the St. James Avenue exit was a small stand that sold sandwiches. I stopped. "How about a sandwich and a cup of coffee, Manfred? On me, any kind. Yogurt too, and an apple if you'd like. My treat."

"I'm not hungry," he said.

"Okay by me," I said. "Hope you don't mind if I dine."

"Why don't you just go dine and stop bothering me?"

"I'll just grab a sandwich here and we'll stroll along, maybe cross the street to the bus terminal, see if any miscegenation is going on or anything."

I bought a tuna on whole wheat, a Winesap apple, and a paper cup of black coffee. I put the apple in my pocket and ate the sandwich as we walked along. At the far end of the arcade, where the Park Square Cinema used to be, we stopped. I had finished my sandwich and was sipping my coffee.

"You still with the Klan, Manfred?"

"Certainly."

"I heard you were regional manager or Grand High Imperial Alligator or whatever for Massachusetts."

He nodded.

"Dynamite," I said, "next step up is playing intermission piano at a child-abuse convention."

"You're a fool, like all the other liberals. Your race will be mongrelized; a culture that took ten thousand years and produced the greatest civilization in history will be lost. Drowned in a sea of half-breeds and savages. Only the Communists will gain."

"Any culture that produced a creep like you, Manfred," I said, "is due for improvement."

"Dupe," he said.

"But I didn't come here to argue ethnic purity with you."

"You'd lose," he said.

"Probably," I said. "You're a professional bigot. You spend your life arguing it. You are an expert. It's your profession. And it ain't mine. I don't spend two hours a month debating racial purity. But even if I lose the argument, I'll win the fight afterwards."

"And you people are always accusing us of violence," Manfred said. He was standing very straight with his back against the wall near the barren area where the advertisements for the Cinema used to be. There was some color on his cheeks.

"*You people*?" I said. "*Us*? I'm talking about me and you. I'm not talking about *us* and about *you people*."

"You don't understand politics," Manfred said. "You can't change society talking about *you* and *me*."

"Manfred, I would like to know something about a group

of people as silly as you are. Calls itself RAM, which stands for Restore American Morality."

"Why ask me?"

"Because you are the kind of small dogturd who hangs around groups like this one and talks about restoring morality. It probably helps you to feel like less of a dogturd."

"I don't know anything about RAM."

"It is opposed to feminism and gay activism—probably in favor of God and racial purity. You must've heard about them?"

Manfred shook his head. He was looking at his feet again. I put my fist under his chin and raised it until he was looking at me. "I want to know about this group, Manfred," I said.

"I promise you, I don't know nothing about them," Manfred said.

"Then you should be sure to find out about them, Manfred."

He tried to twist his chin off my fist, but I increased the upward pressure a little and held him still.

"I don't do your dirty work."

"You do. You do anyone's. You're a piece of shit, and you do what you're told. Just a matter of pressure," I said.

His eyes shifted away from me. Several people coming out of the bank to my right paused and looked at us, and then moved hurriedly along.

"There are several kinds of pressure, Manfred. I can come into work every day and harass you until they fire you. I can go wherever you go and tell them about how we busted you for possession of an inflatable lover, and how you sang like the Mormon Tabernacle Choir to get off." There was more color in his cheeks now. "Or," I said, "I could punch your face into scrapple once a day until you had my information."

With his teeth clenched from the pressure of my fist, Manfred said, "You miserable prick." His whole face was red now. I increased the pressure and brought him up on his toes.

"Vilification," I said. "You people are always vilifying us." I let him go and stepped away from him. "I'll be around tomorrow to see what you can tell me," I said.

"Maybe I won't be here," he said.

"I know where you live, Manfred. I'll find you."

He was still standing very straight and stiff against the wall. His breath was hissing between his teeth. His eyes looked bright to me, feverish.

"Tomorrow, Manfred. I'll be by tomorrow."

18

I WENT OUT to Arlington Street and turned left and walked down to Boylston eating my Winesap apple. On Boylston Street there were lots of Christmas decorations and pictures of Santa Claus and a light, pleasant snow falling. I wondered if Rachel Wallace could see the snow from where she was. 'Tis the season to be jolly. If I had stayed with her. . . . I shook my head. Hard. No point to that. It probably wasn't much more unpleasant to be kidnaped in the Christmas season than any other time. I hadn't stayed with her. And thinking I should have wouldn't help find her. Got to concentrate on the priority items, babe. Got to think about finding her. Automatically, as I went by Brentano's, I stopped and looked in the window at the books. I didn't have much hope for Manfred—he was mean and bigoted and stupid. Cosgrove was none of those things, but he was a working reporter on a liberal newspaper. Anything he found out, he'd have to stumble over. No one was going to tell him.

I finished my apple and dropped the core in a trash basket attached to a lamp post. I looked automatically in Malben's window at the fancy food. Then I could cross and see what new Japanese food was being done at Hai Hai, then back this side and stare at the clothes in Louis, perhaps stop off at the Institute of Contemporary Art. Then I could go home and take a nap. Shit. I walked back to my office and got my car and drove to Belmont.

The snow wasn't sticking as I went along Storrow Drive, and it was early afternoon with no traffic. On my right the Charles was very black and cold-looking. Along the river people jogged in their winter running clothes. A very popular model was longjohns under shorts, with a hooded sweatshirt and blue New Balance shoes with white trim. I preferred a cutoff sweatshirt over black turtleneck sweater, with blue warm-up pants to match the New Balance 320's. Diversity. It made America great.

I crossed the Charles to the Cambridge side near Mt. Auburn Hospital and drove through a slice of Cambridge through Watertown, out Belmont Street to Belmont. The snow was beginning to collect as I pulled into a Mobil station on Trapelo Road and got directions to the Belmont Police Station on Concord Avenue.

I explained to the desk sergeant who I was, and he got so excited at one point that he glanced up at me for a moment before he went back to writing in a spiral notebook.

"I'm looking for one of your patrol car people. Young guy, twenty-five, twenty-six. Five ten, hundred eighty pounds, very cocky, wears military decorations on his uniform blouse. Probably eats raw wolverine for breakfast."

Without looking up the desk sergeant said, "That'd be Foley. Wise mouth."

"Man's gotta make his mark somehow," I said. "Where do I find him?"

The sergeant looked at something official under the counter. "He's cruising up near the reservoir," he said. "I'll have the dispatcher call him. You know the Friendly's up on Trapelo?"

"Yeah, I passed it coming in," I said.

"I'll have him meet you in the parking lot there."

I thanked him and went out and drove up to Friendly's ice cream parlor. Five minutes after I got there, a Belmont cruiser pulled in and parked. I got out of my car in the steady snowfall and walked over to the cruiser and got in the back seat. Foley was driving. His partner was the same older cop with the pot belly, still slouched in the passenger seat with his hat over his eyes.

Foley shifted sideways and grinned at me over the seat. "So someone snatched your lez, huh?"

"How gracefully you put it," I said.

"And you got no idea who, and you come out grabbing straws. You want me to ID the cluck you hit in the gut, don't you?"

I said to the older cop, "How long you figure before he's chief?"

The older cop ignored me.

"Am I right or wrong?"

"Right," I said, "you know who he is?"

"Yeah, after we was all waltzing together over by the library that day, I took down his license number when he drove off, and I checked into him when I had time. Name's English—Lawrence Turnbull English, Junior. Occupation, financial consultant. Means he don't do nothing. Family's got twelve, fifteen million bucks. He consults with their trust officer on how to spend it. That's as much as he works. Spends a lot of time taking the steam, playing racquetball, and protecting democracy from the coons and the queers and the commies and the lower classes, and the libbers and like that."

The old cop shifted a little in the front seat and said, "He's got an IQ around eight, maybe ten."

"Benny's right," Foley said. "He snatched that broad, he'd forget where he hid her."

"Where's he live?" I said.

Foley took a notebook out of his shirt pocket, ripped out a page, and handed it to me. "Watch your ass with him though. Remember, he's a friend of the chief's," Foley said.

"Yeah," I said. "Thanks."

A plow rumbled by on Trapelo Road as I got out of the cruiser and went back to my car. The windows were opaque with snow, and I had to scrape them clean before I could drive. I went into the same Mobil station and got my tank filled and asked for directions to English's house.

It was in a fancy part of Belmont. A rambling, gabled house that looked like one of those old nineteenth century resort hotels. Probably had a hunting preserve in the snow behind it. The plow had tossed up a small drift in front of the driveway, and I had to shove my car through it. The driveway was clear and circled up behind the house to a wide apron in front of a garage with four doors. To the right of the garage there was a back door. I disdained it. I went back around to the front door. A blow for the classless society. A young woman in a maid suit answered the bell. Black dress, little white apron, little hat—just like in the movies.

I said, "Is the master at home?"

She said, "Excuse me?"

I said, "Mr. English? Is he at home?"

"Who shall I say is calling, please?"

"Spenser," I said, "representing Rachel Wallace. We met once, tell him, at the Belmont Library."

The maid said, "Wait here, please," and went off down the hall. She came back in about ninety seconds and said, "This way, please."

We went down the hall and into a small pine-paneled room with a fire on the hearth and a lot of books on built-in shelves on either side of the fireplace. English was sitting in a red-and-gold wing chair near the fire, wearing an honest-to-God smoking jacket with black velvet lapels and smoking a meerschaum pipe. He had on black-rimmed glasses and a book by Harold Robbins was closed in his right hand, the forefinger keeping the place.

He stood up as I came in but did not put out his hand—probably didn't want to lose his place. He said, "What do you want, Mr. Spenser?"

"As you may know, Rachel Wallace was kidnaped yesterday."

"I heard that on the news," he said. We still stood.

"I'm looking for her."

"Yes?"

"Can you help?"

"How on earth could I help?" English said. "What have I to do with her?"

"You picketed her speech at the library. You called her a bulldyke. As I recall, you said you'd 'never let her win' or something quite close to that."

"I deny saying any such thing," English said. "I exercised my Constitutional right of free speech by picketing. I made no threats whatsoever. You assaulted me."

So he hadn't forgotten.

"We don't have to be mad at each other, Mr. English. We can do this easy."

"I wish to do nothing with you. It is preposterous that you'd think I knew anything about a crime."

"On the other hand," I said, "we can do it the other way. We can talk this all over with the Boston cops. There's a sergeant named Belson there who'll be able to choke back the terror he feels when you mention your friend, the chief. He'd feel duty bound to drag your tail over to Berkeley Street and ask you about the reports that you'd threatened Rachel Wallace before witnesses. If you annoyed him, he might even feel it necessary to hold you overnight in the tank with the winos and fags and riffraff."

"My attorney—" English said.

"Oh yeah," I said, "Belson just panics when an attorney shows up. Sometimes he gets so nervous, he forgets where he put the client. And the attorney has to chase all over the metropolitan area with his writ, looking into assorted pens and tanks and getting puke on his Chesterfield overcoat to see if he can find his client."

English opened his mouth and closed it and didn't say anything.

I went and sat in his red-and-gold wing chair. "How'd you know Rachel Wallace was going to be at the library?" I said.

"It was advertised in the local paper," he said.

"Who organized the protest?"

"Well, the committee had a meeting."

"What committee?"

"The vigilance committee."

"I bet I know your motto," I said.

"Eternal vigilance—" he said.

"I know," I said. "I know. Who is the head of the committee?"

"I am chairman."

"Gee, and still so humble," I said.

"Spenser, I do not find you funny," he said.

"Puts you in excellent company," I said. "Could you account for your movements since Monday night at nine o'clock if someone asked you?"

"Of course I could. I resent being asked."

"Go ahead," I said.

"Go ahead what?"

"Go ahead and account for your movements since nine o'clock Monday night."

"I certainly will not. I have no obligation to tell you anything."

"We already did this once, Lawrence. Tell me, tell Belson—I don't care."

"I have absolutely nothing to hide."

"Funny how I knew you'd say that. Too bad to waste it on me though. It'll dazzle the cops."

"Well, I don't," he said. "I don't have anything to hide. I was at a committee meeting from seven thirty Monday night until eleven fifteen. Then I came straight home to bed."

"Anybody see you come home?"

"My mother, several of the servants."

"And the next day?"

"I was at Old Colony Trust at nine fifteen, I left there at

eleven, played racquetball at the club, then lunched at the club. I returned home after lunch, arrived here at three fifteen. I read until dinner. After dinner—"

"Okay, enough. I'll check on all of this, of course. Who'd you play racquetball with?"

"I simply will not involve my friends in this. I will not have you badgering and insulting them."

I let that go. He'd fight that one. He didn't want his friends at the club to know he was being investigated, and a guy like English will dig in to protect his reputation. Besides I could check it easily. The club and the committee, too.

"Badger?" I said. "Insult? Lawrence, how unkind. I am clearly not of your social class, but I am not without grace."

"Are you through?"

"I am for now," I said. "I will authenticate your—if you'll pardon the expression—alibi, and I may look further into your affairs. If the alibi checks, I'll still keep you in mind, however. You didn't have to do it, to have it done, or to know who did it."

"I shall sue you if you continue to bother me," English said.

"And if you are involved in any way in anything that happened to Rachel Wallace," I said, "I will come back and put you in the hospital."

English narrowed his eyes a little. "Are you threatening me?" he said.

"That's exactly it, Lawrence," I said. "That is exactly what I am doing. I am threatening you."

English looked at me with his eyes narrowed for a minute, and then he said, "You'd better leave."

"Okay by me," I said, "but remember what I told you. If you are holding out on me, I'll find out, and I'll come back. If you know something and don't tell me, I will find out, and I will hurt you."

He stood and opened the study door.

"A man in my position has resources, Spenser." He was still squinting at me. I realized that was his tough look.

"Not enough," I said, and walked off down the hall and out the front door. The snow had stopped. Around back, a Plymouth sedan was parked next to my car. When I walked over to it, the window rolled down and Belson looked out at me.

"Thought this was your heap," he said. "Learn anything?"

I laughed. "I just got through threatening English with you," I said, "so he'd talk to me. Now here you are, and he could just as well not have talked to me."

"Get in," Belson said. "We'll compare notes."

I got in the back seat. Belson was in the passenger seat. A cop I didn't know sat behind the wheel. Belson didn't introduce us.

"How'd you get here?" I said.

"You told Quirk about the library scene," Belson said, "and we questioned Linda Smith along with everybody else and she mentioned it to me. I had it on my list when Quirk mentioned it to me. So we called the Belmont Police and found ourselves about an hour behind you. What you get?"

"Not much," I said. "If it checks out, he's got an alibi for all the time that he needs."

"Run it past us," Belson said. "We won't mention you, and we'll see if the story stays the same."

I told Belson what English had told me. The cop I didn't know was writing a few things in a notebook. When I was through, I got out of the Plymouth and into my own car. Through the open window I said to Belson, "Anything surfaces, I'd appreciate hearing."

"Likewise," Belson said.

I rolled up the window and backed out and turned down the drive. As I pulled onto the street I saw Belson and the other cop get out and start toward the front door. The small drift of snow that had blocked the driveway when I'd arrived was gone. Man in English's position was not without resources.

19

THE MAIN ENTRANCE to the Boston Public Library used to face Copley Square across Dartmouth Street. There was a broad exterior stairway and inside there was a beautiful marble staircase leading up to the main reading room with carved lions and high-domed ceilings. It was always a pleasure to go there. It felt like a library and looked like a library, and even when I was going in there to look up Duke Snider's lifetime batting average, I used to feel like a scholar.

Then they grafted an addition on and shifted the main entrance to Boylston Street. *Faithful to the spirit*, the architect had probably said. *But making a contemporary statement*, I bet he said. The addition went with the original like Tab goes with pheasant. Now, even if I went into study the literary influence of Eleanor of Aquitaine, I felt like I'd come out with a pound of hamburger and a loaf of Wonder bread.

By the big glass doors a young woman in Levi's and rabbit fur coat told me she was trying to raise money to get a bus back to Springfield. She had one tooth missing and a bruise on her right cheekbone. I didn't give her anything.

I went through the new part to the old and walked around a bit and enjoyed it, and then I went to the periodical section and started looking at the *Globe* on microfilm to see what I could find out about the Belmont Vigilance Committee. I was there all day. Next to me a fragrant old geezer in a long overcoat slept with his head resting on the microfilm viewer in front of him. The overcoat was buttoned up to his neck even though the room was hot. No one bothered him.

At noon I went out and went across the street to a Chinese restaurant and ate some Peking ravioli and some mushu pork for lunch. When I went back for the afternoon session the old man was gone, but the broad with the missing tooth was still working the entrance. At five o'clock I had seven pages of notes, and my eyes were starting to cross. If I weren't so tough, I would have thought about reading glasses. I wonder how Bogie would have looked with specs. Here's looking at you, four-eyes. I shut off the viewer, returned the last microfilm cassette, put on my coat, and went out to a package store, where I bought two bottles of Asti Spumante.

I was driving up to Smithfield to have dinner with Susan, and the traffic northbound was stationary a long way back onto Storrow Drive. I deked and dived up over the Hill and down across Cambridge Street past the Holiday Inn, behind Mass. General and got to the traffic light at Leverett Circle almost as quick as the people who just sat in line on Storrow. The radio traffic-reporter told me from his helicopter that there was a "fender-bender" on the bridge, so I turned off onto 93 and went north that way. A magician with the language—*fender-bender*, wow! It was six when I turned off of Route 128 at the Main Street-Smithfield exit. Out in the subs most of the snow was still white. There were candles in all the windows and wreaths on all the doors, and some people had Santas on their rooftops, and some people had colored lights on their shrubbery. One house had a drunken Santa clutching a bottle of Michelob under the disapproving stare of a red-nosed reindeer. Doubtless the antichrist lurks in the subs as well.

Susan's house had a spotlight on the front and a sprig of white pine hanging on the brass doorknocker. I parked in her driveway and walked to her front door, and she opened it before I got there.

"Fa-la-la-la-la," I said.

She leaned against the doorjamb and put one hand on her hip.

"Hey, Saint Nick," she said, "you in town long?"

"Trouble with you Jews," I said, "is that you mock our Christian festivals."

She gave me a kiss and took the wine, and I followed her in. There was a fire in her small living room and on the coffee table some caponata and triangles of Syrian bread. There was a good cooking smell mixed with the wood-smoke. I sniffed. "Onions," I said, "and peppers."

"Yes," she said, "and mushrooms. And rice pilaf. And when the fire burns down and the coals are right, you can grill two steaks, and we'll eat."

"And then?" I said.

"Then maybe some Wayne King albums on the stereo and waltz till dawn."

"Can we dip?"

"Certainly, but you have to wait for the music. No dipping before it starts. Want a beer?"

"I know where," I said.

"I'll say."

"White wine and soda for you?"

She nodded. I got a bottle of Beck's out of her poppy-red refrigerator and poured white wine from a big green jug into a tall glass. I put in ice, soda, and a twist of lime, and gave it to her. We went back into the living room and sat on her couch, and I put my arm around her shoulder and laid my head back against the couch and closed my eyes.

"You look like the dragon won today," she said.

"No, didn't even see one. I spent the day in the BPL looking at microfilm."

She sipped her wine and soda. "You freebooters do have an adventurous life, don't you?" With her left hand she reached up and touched my left hand as it rested on her shoulder.

"Well, some people find the search for truth exciting."

"Did you find some?" she said.

"Some," I said. Susan drew a series of small circles on the back of my hand with her forefinger. "Or at least some facts. Truth is a little harder, maybe."

I took a small triangle of Syrian bread and picked up some caponata with it and ate it and drank some beer.

"It's hard to hug and eat simultaneously," I said.

"For you that may be the definition of a dilemma," she said.

She sipped at her wine. I finished my beer. A log on the fire settled. I heaved myself off the couch and went to the kitchen for more beer. When I came back, I stood in the archway between the living room and dining room and looked at her.

She had on a white mannish-looking shirt of oxford cloth with a button-down collar, and an expensive brown skirt and brown leather boots, the kind that wrinkle at the ankles. Her feet were up on the coffee table. Around her neck two thin gold chains showed where the shirt was open. She wore them almost all the time. She had on big gold earrings; her face was thoroughly made up. There were fine lines around her eyes, and her black hair shone. She watched me looking at her. There stirred behind her face a sense of life and purpose and mirth and caring that made her seem to be in motion even as she was still. There was a kind of rhythm to her, even in motionless repose. I said, "Energy contained by grace, maybe."

She said, "I beg your pardon?"

I said, "I was just trying to find a phrase to describe the quality you have of festive tranquility."

"That's an oxymoron," she said.

"Well, it's not my fault," I said.

"You know damn well what an oxymoron is," she said. "I just wanted you to know that I know."

"You know everything you need to," I said.

"Sit down," she said, "and tell me what you found out in the library."

I sat beside her, put my feet up beside hers and my arm back around her shoulder, leaned my head back on the couch, closed my eyes, and said, "I found out that the Belmont Vigilance Committee is a somewhat larger operation that I would have thought. It was founded during the Korean war by English's father to combat the clear menace of Communist subversion in this country. Old man English managed to stave off the commies until his death in 1965, at which time the family business, which as far as I can tell is anti-Communism, passed into the hands of his only son, Lawrence Turnbull English, Jr. There was a daughter, Geraldine Julia English, but she went off to Goucher College and then got married and dropped out of things. Probably got radicalized in college, mixing with all those com-symp professors. Anyway there's Lawrence Junior, Harvard '61, and his momma, who looks like Victor McLaglen, living in the old homestead, with fifteen million or so to keep them from the cold, running the committee and spreading the gospel and opening new chapters and stamping out sedition as fast as it springs up. The committee has chapters in most of the metropolitan colleges, some high schools, and most neighborhoods across the Commonwealth. Ninety-six chapters by last count, which was 1977. They sprung up like toadstools in the Boston neighborhoods when busing was hot. There's chapters in South Boston, Dorchester, Hyde Park, all over. Lawrence Junior was right there on the barricades when the buses rolled into South Boston High. He got arrested once for obstructing traffic and once for failing to obey the lawful order of a policeman. Both times his mom had someone down to post bond by the time the wagon got to the jail. Second time he filed suit alleging police brutality on the part of a big statie from Fitchburg named Thomas J. Fogarty, who apparently helped him into the wagon with the front end of his right boot. Case was dismissed."

"And that's what English does? Run the Vigilance Committee."

"I only know what I read in the papers," I said. "If they

are right, that seems to be the case. A real patriot. Keeping his fifteen million safe from the reds."

"And the daughter isn't involved?"

"There's nothing about her. Last entry was about her marriage to some guy from Philadelphia in 1968. She was twenty."

"What's she do now?" Susan said. She was making her circles on the back of my hand again.

"I don't know. Why do you care?"

"I don't—I was just curious. Trying to be interested in your work, cookie."

"It's a woman's role," I said.

She said, "I spent the day talking to the parents of learning-disabled children."

"Is that educatorese for dummies?"

"Oh, you sensitive devil. No, it isn't. It's kids with dyslexia, for instance—that sort of thing."

"How were the parents?"

"Well, the first one wanted to know if this had to go on his record. The kid is in the eleventh grade and can't really read.

"I said that I wasn't sure what she meant about the record. And she said if it were on his record that the kid was dyslexic, wouldn't that adversely affect his chances of going to a good college."

"Least she's got her priorities straight," I said.

"And the next mother—the fathers don't usually come—the next mother said it was our job to teach the kid, and she was sick of hearing excuses."

I said, "I think I might have had a better time in the library."

She said, "The coals look pretty good. Would you like to handle the steaks?"

"Where does it say that cooking steaks is man's work?" I said.

Her eyes crinkled and her face brightened. "Right above the section on what sexual activity one can look forward to after steak and mushrooms."

"I'll get right on the steaks," I said.

20

SUSAN WENT TO work in the bright, new-snow suburban morning just before eight. I stayed and cleaned up last night's dishes and made the bed and took a shower. There was no point banging heads with commuter traffic.

At eleven minutes after ten I walked into the arcade of the Park Square Building to talk with Manfred Roy. He wasn't there. The head man at the barber shop told me that Manfred had called in sick and was probably home in bed.

I said, "He still living down on Commonwealth Avenue?"

The barber said, "I don't know where he lives."

I said, "Probably does. I'll stop by and see how he is."

The barber shrugged and went back to trimming a neat semi-circle around some guy's ear. I went out and strolled down Berkeley Street two blocks to Commonwealth. When we had first put the arm on Manfred, he was living on the river side, near the corner of Dartmouth Street. I walked up the mall toward the address. The snow on the mall was still clean and fresh from the recent fall. The mall walkway had been cleared and people were walking their dogs along it. Three kids were playing Frisbee and drinking Miller's beer out of clear glass bottles. A woman with a bull terrier walked by. The terrier had on a plaid doggie sweater and was straining at his leash. I thought his little piggie eyes looked very embarrassed, but that was probably anthropomorphism.

At the corner of Dartmouth Street I stopped and waited for the light. Across the street in front of Manfred's apartment four men were sitting in a two-tone blue Pontiac Bonneville. One of them rolled down the window and yelled across the street, "Your name Spenser?"

"Yeah," I said, "S-p-e-n-s-e-r, like the English poet."

"We want to talk with you," he said.

"Jesus," I said, "I wish I'd thought of saying that."

They piled out of the car. The guy that talked was tall and full of sharp corners, like he'd been assembled from Lego blocks. He had on a navy watch cap and a plaid lumberman's jacket and brown pants that didn't get to the tops of his black shoes. His coat sleeves were too short and his knobby wrists stuck out. His hands were very large with angular knuckles. His jaw moved steadily on something, and as he crossed the street he spat tobacco juice.

The other three were all heavy and looked like men who'd done heavy labor for a long time. The shortest of them had slightly bowed legs, and there was scar tissue thick around his eyes. His nose was thicker than it should have been. I had some of those symptoms myself, and I knew where he got them. Either he hadn't quit as soon as I had or he'd lost more fights. His face looked like a catcher's mitt.

The four of them gathered in front of me on the mall. "What are you doing around here?" the tall one said.

"I'm taking a species count on maggots," I said. "With you four and Manfred I got five right off."

The bow-legged pug said, "He's a smart guy, George. Lemme straighten him out."

George shook his head. He said to me, "You're looking for trouble, you're going to get it. We don't want you bothering Manfred."

"You in the Klan, too?" I said.

"We ain't here to talk, pal," George said.

"You must be in the Klan," I said. "You're a smooth talker and a slick dresser. Where's Manfred—his mom won't let him come out?"

The pug put his right hand flat on my chest and shoved me about two steps backwards. "Get out of here or we'll stomp the shit out of you," he said. He was slow. I hit him two left jabs and a right hook before he even got his hands up. He sat down in the snow.

"No wonder your face got marked up so bad," I said to him. "You got no reflexes."

There was a small smear of blood at the base of the pug's nostrils. He wiped the back of his hand across and climbed to his feet.

"You gonna get it now," he said.

George made a grab at me, and I hit him in the throat. He rocked back. The other two jumped, and the three of us went down in the snow. Someone hit me on the side of the head. I got the heel of my hand under someone's nose and rammed upward. The owner of the nose cried out in pain. George kicked me in the ribs with his steel-toed work shoes. I rolled away, stuck my fingers in someone's eyes, and rolled up onto my feet. The pug hit me a good combination as I was moving past. If I'd been moving toward him, it would have put me down. One of them jumped on my back. I reached up, got hold of his hair, doubled over, and pulled with his momentum. He went over my shoulder and landed on his back on a park bench. The pug hit me on the side of the jaw and I stumbled. He hit me again, and I rolled away from it and lunged against George. He wrapped his arms around me and tried to hold me. I brought both fists up to the level of his ears and pounded them together with his head in between. He grunted and his grip relaxed. I broke free of him and someone hit me with something larger than a fist and the inside of my head got loud and red and I went down.

When I opened my eyes there were granules of snow on the lashes; they looked like magnified salt crystals. There was no sound and no movement. Then there was a snuffing sound. I rolled my eyes to the left, and over the small rim of snow I could see a black nose with slight pink outlinings. It snuffed at me. I shifted my head slightly and said, "*Uff*." The nose pulled back. It was on one end of a dog, an apprehensive young Dalmatian that stood with its front legs stiffened and its hindquarters raised and its tail making uncertain wags.

Lifting my head was too hard. I put it back in the snow. The dog moved closer and snuffed at me again. I heard someone yell, "Digger!" The dog shuffled his feet uncertainly.

Someone yelled, "Digger!" again, and the dog moved away. I took a deep breath. It hurt my ribcage. I exhaled, inhaled again, inched my arms under me, and pushed myself up onto my hands and knees. My head swam. I felt my stomach tighten, and I threw up, which hurt the ribs some more. I stayed that way for a bit, on my hands and knees with my head hanging, like a winded horse. My eyes focused a little better. I could see the snow and the dog's footprints, beyond them the legs of a park bench. I crawled over, got hold of it, and slowly got myself upright. Everything blurred for a minute, then came back into focus again. I inhaled some more and felt a little steadier. I looked around. The mall was empty. The Dalmatian was a long way down the mall now, walking with a man and woman. The snow where I stood was trampled and churned. There was a lot of blood spattered on the snow. Across the street in front of Manfred's apartment the Pontiac was gone. I felt my mouth with my left hand. It was swollen, but no teeth were loose. My nose seemed okay, too.

I let go of the bench and took a step. My ribs were stiff and sore. My head ached. I had to wait for a moment while dizziness came and went. I touched the back of my head. It was swollen and wet with blood. I took a handful of snow from the bench seat and held it against the swollen part. Then I took another step, and another. I was under way. My apartment was three blocks away—one block to Marlborough Street, two blocks down toward the Public Garden. I figured I'd make it by sundown.

Actually I made it before sundown. It wasn't quite noon when I let myself in and locked the door behind me. I took two aspirin with a glass of milk, made some black coffee, added a large shot of Irish whiskey and a teaspoon of sugar, and sipped it while I got undressed. I examined myself in the bathroom mirror. One eye was swollen and my lower lip was puffy. There was a seeping lump on the back of my head and a developing bruise that was going to be a lulu on my right side. But the ribs didn't appear to be broken, and in fact there seemed to be nothing but surface damage. I took a long hot shower and put on clean clothes and had some more coffee and whiskey, and cooked myself two lambchops for lunch. I ate the lambchops with black bread, drank some more coffee with whiskey, and cleaned up the kitchen. I felt lousy but alive, and my fourth cup of whiskeyed coffee made me feel less lousy.

I looked into the bedroom at my bed and thought about lying down for a minute and decided not to. I took out my gun and spun the cylinder, made sure everything worked smoothly, put the gun back in my hip holster again, and went back out of my apartment.

I walked the three blocks back to Manfred's place a lot faster than I had walked from Manfred's two hours earlier. I was not sprightly, but I was moving steadily along.

21

WHEN I RANG the bell Manfred's mom came to the door. She was thin and small, wearing a straight striped dress and white sneakers with a hole cut in one of them to relieve pressure on a bunion. Her hair was short and looked as if it had been trimmed with a jackknife. Her face was small, and all the features were clustered in the middle of it. She wore no make-up.

I said, "Good afternoon, ma'am. Is Manfred Roy here, please?"

She looked at my face uneasily. "He's having his lunch," she said. Her voice was very deep.

I stepped partway into the apartment and said, "I'll be glad to wait, ma'am. Tell him I have some good news about Spenser."

She stood uncertainly in the doorway. I edged a little further into the apartment. She edged back a little.

Manfred called from another room, "Who is it, Ma?"

"Man says he has good news about Spenser," she said. I smiled at her benignly. Old Mr. Friendly.

Manfred appeared in the archway to my right. He had a napkin tucked in his belt and a small milk mustache on his upper lip. When he saw me, he stopped dead.

"The good news is that I'm not badly hurt, good buddy," I said. "Ain't that swell?"

Manfred backed up a step. "I don't know nothing about that, Spenser."

"About what?" his mother said. I edged all the way past her.

"About what, Manfred?" I said. His mom still stood with one hand on the doorknob.

"I didn't have nothing to do with you getting beat up."

"I'll not be able to say the same about you, Manfred."

Mrs. Roy said, "What do you want here? You said you had good news. You lied to get in here."

"True," I said. "I did lie. But if I hadn't lied, sort of, then you wouldn't have let me in, and I'd have had to kick in your door. I figured the lie was cheaper."

"Don't you threaten my mother," Manfred said.

"No, I won't. It's you I came to threaten, Manfred."

Mrs. Roy said, "Manfred, I'm going for the police," and started out into the hall.

"No, Ma. Don't do that," Manfred said. Mrs. Roy stopped in the hall and looked back in at him. Her eyes were sick.

"Why shouldn't I go to the police, Manfred?"

"They wouldn't understand," Manfred said. "He'd lie to them. They'd believe him. I'd get in trouble."

"Are you from the niggers?" she said to me.

"I represent a woman named Rachel Wallace, Mrs. Roy. She was kidnaped. I think your son knows something about it. I spoke to him about it yesterday and said I'd come visit him today. This morning four men who knew my name and recognized me on sight were parked in a car outside your apartment. When I arrived, they beat me up."

Mrs. Roy's eyes looked sicker—a sickness that must have gone back a long way. A lifetime of hearing hints that her son wasn't right. That he didn't get along. That he was in trouble or around it. A lifetime of odd people coming to the door and Manfred hustling in and out and not saying exactly what was up. A lifetime sickness of repressing the almost-sure knowledge that your firstborn was very wrong.

"I didn't have nothing to do with that, Ma. I don't know nothing about a kidnaping. Spenser just likes to come and push me around. He knows I don't like his nigger friends. Well, some of my friends don't like him pushing me around."

"My boy had nothing to do with any of that," Mrs. Roy said. Her voice was guttural with tension.

"Then you ought to call the cops, Mrs. Roy. I'm trespassing. And I won't leave."

Mrs. Roy didn't move. She stood with one foot in the hall and one foot in the apartment.

Manfred turned suddenly and ran back through the archway. I went after him. To the left was the kitchen, to the right a short corridor with two doors off it. Manfred went through the nearest one, and when I reached him, he had a short automatic pistol halfway out of the drawer of a bedside table. With the heel of my right fist I banged the drawer shut on his hand. He cried out once. I took the back of his shirt with my left hand and yanked him back toward me and into the hall, spinning him across my body and slamming him against the wall opposite the bedroom door. Then I took the gun out of the drawer. It was a Mauser HSc, a 7.65mm pistol that German pilots used to carry in World War II.

I took the clip out, ran the action back to make sure there was nothing in the chamber, and slipped the pistol in my hip pocket.

Manfred stood against the wall sucking on the bruised fingers of his right hand. His mother had come down the hall and stood beside him, her hands at her side. "What did he take from you?" she said to Manfred.

I took the pistol out. "This, Mrs. Roy. It was in a drawer beside the bed."

"It's for protection, Ma."

"You got a license for this, Manfred?"

"Course I do."

"Lemme see it."

"I don't have to show you. You're not on the cops no more."

"You don't have a permit do you, Manfred?" I smiled a big smile. "You know what the Massachusetts handgun law says?"

"I got a license."

"The Massachusetts handgun law provides that anyone convicted of the possession of an unlicensed handgun gets a mandatory one-year jail sentence. Sentence may not be suspended nor parole granted. That's a year in the joint, Manfred."

"Manfred, do you have a license?" his mother said.

He shook his head. All four fingers of his bruised right hand were in his mouth and he sucked at them.

Mrs. Roy looked at me. "Don't tell," she said.

"Ever been in the joint, Manfred?"

With his fingers still in his mouth Manfred shook his head.

"They do a lot of bad stuff up there, Manfred. Lot of homosexuality. Lot of hatred. Small blond guys tend to be in demand."

"Don't tell," his mother said. She had moved between me and Manfred. Manfred's eyes were squeezed nearly shut. There were tears in the corners.

I smiled my nice big smile at his mother. Old Mr. Friendly. Here's how your kid's going to get raped in the slammer, ma'am.

"Maybe we can work something out," I said. "See, I'm looking for Rachel Wallace. If you gave me any help on that, I'd give you back your Mauser and speak no ill of you to the fuzz."

I was looking at Manfred but I was talking for his mother, too.

"I don't know nothing about it," Manfred mumbled around his fingers. He seemed to have shrunk in on himself, as if his stomach hurt.

I shook my head sadly. "Talk to him, Mrs. Roy. I don't want to have to put him away. I'm sure you need him here to look after you."

Mrs. Roy's face was chalky, and the lines around her mouth and eyes were slightly reddened. She was beginning to breathe hard, as if she'd been running. Her mouth was open a bit, and I noticed that her front teeth were gone.

"You do what he says, Manfred. You help this man like he says." She didn't look at Manfred as she talked. She stood between him and me and looked at me.

I didn't say anything. None of us did. We stood nearly still in the small hallway. Manfred snuffed a little. Some pipes knocked.

Still looking at me, with Manfred behind her, Mrs. Roy said, "God damn you to hell, you little bastard, you do what this man says. You're in trouble. You've always been in trouble. Thirty years old and you still live with your mother and never go out of the house except to those crazy meetings. Whyn't you leave the niggers alone? Whyn't you let the government take care of them? Whyn't you get a good job or get an education or get a woman or get the hell out the house once in awhile, and not get in trouble? Now this man's going to put you in jail unless you do what he says, and you better the hell damn well goddamned do it." She was crying by the time she got halfway through, and her ugly little face looked a lot worse.

And Manfred was crying. "Ma," he said.

I smiled as hard as I could, my big friendly smile. The Yuletide spirit. 'Tis the season to be jolly.

"All my life," she said. Now she was sobbing, and she turned and put her arms around him. "All my rotten goddamn life I've been saddled with you and you've been queer and awful and I've worried all about you by myself and no man in the house."

"Ma," Manfred said, and they both cried full out.

I felt awful.

"I'm looking for Rachel Wallace," I said. "I'm going to find her. Anything that I need to do, I'll do."

"Ma," Manfred said. "Don't, Ma. I'll do what he says. Ma, don't."

I crossed my arms and leaned on the doorjamb and looked at Manfred. It was not easy to do. I wanted to cry, too.

"What do you want me to do, Spenser?"

"I want to sit down and have you tell me anything you've heard or can guess or have imagined about who might have taken Rachel Wallace."

"I'll try to help, but I don't know nothing."

"We'll work on that. Get it together, and we'll sit down and talk. Mrs. Roy, maybe you could make us some coffee."

She nodded. The three of us walked back down the hall. Me last. Mrs. Roy went to the kitchen. Manfred and I went to the living room. The furniture was brightly colored imitation velvet with a lot of antimacassars on the arms. The antimacassars were the kind you buy in Woolworth's, not the kind anyone ever made at home. There was a big new color TV set in one corner of the room.

I sat in one of the bright fuzzy chairs. It was the color of a Santa Claus suit. Manfred stood in the archway. He still had his napkin tucked into his belt.

"What you want to know?" he said.

"Who do you think took Rachel Wallace?" I said. "And where do you think she is?"

"Honest to God, Spenser, I got no idea."

"What is the most anti-feminist group you know of?"

"Anti-feminist?"

"Yeah. Who hates women's lib the most?"

"I don't know about any group like that."

"What do you know about RAM, which stands for Restore American Morality?" I said. I could hear Manfred's mom in the kitchen messing with cookware.

"I never heard of it."

"How about the Belmont Vigilance Committee?"

"Oh, sure, that's Mr. English's group. We coordinated some of the forced-busing tactics with them."

"You know English?"

"Oh, yes. Very wealthy, very important man. He worked closely with us."

"How tough is he?"

"He will not retreat in the face of moral decay and godless Communism."

"Manfred, don't make a speech at me—I'm too old to listen to horseshit. I want to know if he's got the balls to kidnap someone, or if he's crazy enough. Or if he's got the contacts to have someone do it."

"Mr. English wouldn't hesitate to do the right thing," Manfred said.

"Would he know how to arrange a kidnaping?" I said. "And don't give me all that canned tripe in the answer."

Manfred nodded.

"Who would do it for him?" I said.

Manfred shook his head. "I don't know any names, I promise I don't. I just see him with people, and, you know, they're the kind that would know about that kind of stuff."

Mrs. Roy brought in some instant coffee in white mugs that had pictures of vegetables on them. She'd put some Oreo cookies on a plate and she put the two cups and the plate down on a yellow plastic molded coffee table with a translucent plastic top that had been finished to imitate frosted glass.

I said, "Thank you, Mrs. Roy."

Manfred didn't look at her. She didn't look at him, either. She nodded her head at me to acknowledge the thanks and went back to the kitchen. She didn't want to hear what Manfred was saying.

"I heard he could get anything done and that he was a

good man if you needed anything hard done, or you needed to hire anyone for special stuff."

"Like what?" I sipped at the coffee. The water had been added to the coffee before it was hot enough, and the coffee wasn't entirely dissolved. I swallowed and put the cup down.

"You know."

"No, I don't, Manfred. Like what?"

"Well, if you needed people for, like, you know, like fighting and getting things done."

"Like the baboons that pounded on me this morning?"

"I didn't hire them, Spenser. They're from the organization. They wanted to make sure I wasn't bothered."

"Because you are a Klan mucky-muck?" I said. "Second Assistant Lizard?"

"I'm an official. And they were looking out for me. We stick together."

Manfred's voice tried for dignity, but he kept staring at the floor, and dignity is hard, while you're looking at the floor.

"Ever meet his mother or his sister?"

"No."

"Know anything about them?"

"No."

"Manfred, you are not being a help."

"I'm trying, Spenser. I just don't know nothing. I never heard of Rachel Whosis."

"Wallace," I said. "Rachel Wallace."

22

MANFRED AND I chatted for another hour with no better results. Hardly seemed worth getting beat up for. When I left, Mrs. Roy didn't come to say goodbye, and Manfred didn't offer to shake hands. I got even—I didn't wish them Merry Christmas.

It was a little after three when I got back out onto Commonwealth. The whiskey and aspirin had worn off, and I hurt. A three-block walk and I could be in bed, but that wouldn't be looking for Rachel Wallace. That would be taking a nap. Instead I walked down to Berkeley and up three blocks to Police Headquarters to talk with Quirk.

He was there and so was Belson. Quirk had his coat off and his sleeves rolled up. He was squeezing one of those little red rubber grip strengtheners with indentations for the fingers. He did ten in one hand and switched it to the other and did ten more.

"Trying to keep your weight down, Marty?" I said.

Quirk switched the grip strengthener back to his right hand. "Your face looks good," he said.

"I bumped into a door," I said.

"About fifteen times," Belson said. "You come in to make a complaint?"

I shook my head. It made my face hurt. "I came by to see how you guys are making out looking for Rachel Wallace."

"We got shit," Quirk said.

"Anything on those license-tag numbers I gave you?"

Quirk nodded. "The Buick belongs to a guy named Swisher Cody. Used to be a big basketball star at Hyde Park High in the Fifties, where he got the nickname. Dodge belongs to a broad named Mary Stevenson. Says she lets her boyfriend use it all the time. Boyfriend's name is Michael Mulready. He's a pal of Swisher's. They both tell us that they were together the night you say they tried to run you off the road and that they were playing cards with Mulready's cousin Mingo at his place in Watertown. Mingo says that's right. Cody's done time for loansharking. Mingo, too."

"So you let them go," I said.

Quirk shrugged. "Even if we didn't believe them and we believe you, what have we got them for? Careless driving? We let 'em go and we put a tail on them."

"And?"

"And nothing. They both go to work in the Sears warehouse in Dorchester. They stop on the way home for a few beers. They go to bed. Sometimes they drive out to Watertown and play cards with Cousin Mingo."

I nodded. "How about English?"

Quirk nodded at Belson.

Belson said, "Pretty much what you heard. He's chairman of the Vigilance Committee."

"Eternal vigilance is the price of liberty," Quirk said, and squeezed his grip exerciser hard so that the muscles in his forearm looked like suspension cables.

Belson said, "Spenser been lending you books again, Marty?"

Quirk shook his head. "Naw, my kid's taking U.S. History. He's almost as smart as Spenser."

"Maybe he'll straighten out," I said. "What else you got on English?"

Belson shrugged. "Nothing you don't know. He's got money—he thinks it makes him important, and he's probably right. He's got the IQ of a fieldmouse. And he's got an alibi to cover any time Rachel Wallace might have been kidnaped. Did you meet his mother?"

"No. I've seen her picture."

"Ain't she a looker?" He looked at Quirk. "We ever have to bust her, Marty, I want you to send some hard-ass kids from the tac squad. You and me'd get hurt."

"She as nice as she looks?" I said.

"Nowhere near that nice," Belson said. "She sat in while we questioned sonny and tended to answer whatever we asked him. I told her finally, why didn't she hold him on her knee and he could move his lips? She told me she'd see to it that I never worked for any police department in this state."

"You scared?" I said.

"Hell, no," Belson said. "I'm relieved. I thought she was going to kill me."

"She active in the committee?" I said.

"She didn't say," Belson said, "but I'd guess yes. I have the feeling she's active in anything sonny is active in. He doesn't get a hard-on without checking with her."

"You run any check on the family? There's a sister."

Quirk said, "What the hell do you think we do in here —make up Dick Tracy Crimestoppers? Of course we ran a check on the family. Sister's name is Geraldine."

"I know that, for crissake—Geraldine Julia English, Goucher College class of '68."

Quirk went on as if I hadn't said anything. "Geraldine Julia English. Married a guy named Walton Wells in June, 1968, divorced 1972. Works as a model in Boston."

"Wells," I said.

"Yeah, Walton Wells—slick name, huh?"

"Geraldine Julia Wells would be her married name."

Belson said, "You were wrong, Marty. Your kid couldn't be nearly as smart as Spenser."

"What model agency she with?"

Belson said, "Carol Cobb."

"She use her married name?"

"Yeah."

"And her middle name instead of her first, I bet."

Quirk said, "Nobody could be nearly as smart as Spenser."

"She bills herself as Julie Wells, doesn't she?"

Belson nodded.

"Gentlemen," I said, "what we have here is your basic clue. Julie Wells, who is Lawrence Turnbull English, Junior's, sister, was intimate with Rachel Wallace."

"Intimate intimate or just friendly intimate," Quirk said.

"Intimate intimate," I said.

"How do you know this?" Quirk said.

I told him.

"Nice you told us first thing," Quirk said. "Nice you mentioned her name at the beginning of the investigation so we could follow up every possible lead. Very nice." There was no amusement in Quirk's voice now.

"I should have told you," I said. "I was wrong."

"You bet your ass you were wrong," Quirk said. "Being wrong like that tends to put your balls in the fire, too—you know that?"

"You're not the Holy Ghost, Quirk. None of you guys are. I don't have to run in and report everything I know to you every day. I made a guess that this broad was okay, and I didn't want to smell up her rose garden by dragging her into this. Can't you see the *Herald American* headline?

LESBIAN LOVER SUSPECT IN KIDNAPING."

"And maybe you guessed wrong, hot shot, and maybe your girl friend Rachel is dead and gone because you didn't tell us something."

"Or maybe it doesn't mean a goddamned thing," I said. "Maybe you're making a big goddamned event out of nothing." I was leaning back in my chair, one foot propped against the edge of Quirk's desk. He leaned over and slapped the foot away.

"And get your goddamned foot off my desk," he said.

I stood up and so did Quirk.

"Dynamite," Belson said. "You guys fight to the death, and the winner gets to look for Rachel Wallace." He scratched a wooden match on the sole of his shoe and lit a new cigar.

Still standing, Quirk said, "How much do you pay for those goddamned weeds anyway?"

Between puffs to get the cigar going Belson said, "Fifteen cents apiece."

Quirk sat down. "You get screwed," he said.

"They're cheap," Belson said, "but they smell bad."

I sat down.

Quirk said, "Okay. Julie Wells is a member of the English family." He was leaning back now in his swivel chair, his head tipped, staring up at the ceiling, his hands resting on the arms. The rubber grip squeezer lay on the nearly empty desk in front of him. "She is also an intimate of Rachel Wallace. Which means she's gay or at least bisexual." I put one foot up on Quirk's desk again. "Her brother on the other hand is out picketing Rachel Wallace and calling her a dyke and telling her she's immoral and must be stopped," Quirk said.

"We have here a family conflict," Belson said. "And at least an odd coincidence."

"It could be only that," I said.

Quirk's eyes came down from the ceiling and he let the swivel chair come forward until his feet touched the floor.

"It could be," he said. "But it don't do us a lot of good to assume that it is."

"We better get together on how we're going to handle this," I said. "We don't want to charge in and hit her with it, do we?"

"You had your chance to get together with us on this, hot shot, and you didn't take it. We'll decide how to handle it."

"You want to teach me a lesson, Quirk," I said, "or you want to find Rachel Wallace?"

"Both," he said. "Take a walk."

"How about an address for Cody and Mulready?"

"Blow," Quirk said.

I toyed with saying, "I shall return." Figured it was not appropriate and left without a word. As I left Belson blew a smoke ring at me.

23

I WENT HOME feeling lousy. My face hurt, so did my ribs. I'd been making people mad at me all day. I needed someone to tell me I was swell. I called Susan. She wasn't home. I had a bottle of Molson ale, took two aspirin, made a meatloaf sandwich with lettuce, ate it, drank two more ales with it, and went to bed. I dreamed I was locked in a castle room and Susan kept walking by and smiling when I yelled for help. I woke up mad at her, at five minutes of seven in the morning.

When I got up, I forgot about being mad at Susan. I was mad at my body. I could barely walk. I clanked over to the bathroom, and got under the hot water in the shower, and stretched a little while the hot water ran over me. I was in there for maybe half an hour, and when I got out I had cornbread and country sausage and broiled tomato for breakfast and read the *Globe*. Then I put on my gun and went looking for Mulready and Cody.

It was snowing again as I drove on the Southeast Expressway to Dorchester, and the wind was blowing hard so that the snow swirled and eddied in the air. I was going against the commuter rush, but still the traffic was slow, cautious in the snowfall. I slithered off the exit ramp at the big Sears warehouse, stopped at the guard shack, got directions to the main pick-up point, and drove to it.

Quirk had been childish not to give me the addresses. He'd already mentioned that they worked at the Sears warehouse, and he knew I'd go out and find them that way. Immature. Churlish.

I turned up the fleece collar of my jacket before I got out of the car. I put on a blue navy watch cap and a pair of sunglasses. I checked myself in the rearview mirror. Unrecognizable. One of my cleverest disguises. I was impersonating a man dressed for winter. I got out and walked to the warehouse pick-up office.

"Swisher or Michael around?" I said to the young woman behind the call desk.

"Cody and Mulready?"

I nodded.

"They're out back. I can call them on the horn here."

"Yeah, would ya? Tell them Mingo's out here."

She said into the microphone, "Swisher Cody, Michael Mulready, please report to the call desk. A Mr. Mingo is here."

There were three other people in the call office, two of them men. I stood behind the others as we waited. In less than two minutes two men came through the swinging doors behind the desk and glanced around the room. One of them was tall with a big red broken-veined nose and long sideburns. His short hair was reddish with a sprinkling of gray. The other man was much younger. He had blow-dried black hair, a thick black mustache, and a seashell necklace tight around his throat. Contemporary.

I said, "Hey, Swisher."

The tall one with the red hair turned first, then they both looked at me.

"I got a message for you guys from Mingo," I said. "Can you come around?"

Mustache started toward the hinged end of the counter and Red Hair stopped him. He said something I couldn't hear, then they both looked at me again. Then Mustache said something I couldn't hear, then they both bolted through the swinging doors back into the warehouse. So much for my disguise wizardry.

I said, "Excuse me," to the woman waiting for her pick-up and vaulted the counter.

The young lady behind the counter said, "Sir, you can't . . ."

I was through the swinging doors and into the warehouse. There were vast aisles of merchandise and down the center aisle Cody and Mulready were hot-footing it to the rear. The one with the mustache, Mulready, was a step or two behind Cody. I only needed one. I caught them as they were fumbling with a door that said Emergency Only. Cody had it open when I took Mulready from behind. Cody went on out into the snow. I dragged Mulready back.

He turned and tried to knee me in the groin. I turned my hip into his body and blocked him. I got a good grip of shirt front with both hands and pressed him up and backwards until his feet were off the ground and his back was against the wall beside the door. The door had a pneumatic closer and swung slowly shut. I put my face close up to Mulready's and said, "You really got a cousin named Mingo Mulready?"

"What the fuck's wrong with you?" he said. "Lemme the fuck down. What are you, crazy?"

"You know what I'm doing, Michael baby," I said. "You know 'cause you ran when you recognized me."

"I don't know you. Lemme the fuck down."

I banged him once, hard, against the wall.

"You tried to run me and Rachel Wallace off the road a while ago in Lynn. I'm looking for Rachel Wallace, and I'm going to find her, and I don't mind if I have to break things to do it."

Behind me I could hear footsteps coming at a trot. Someone yelled, "Hey, you!"

I pulled Mulready away from the wall and banged him against the safety bar on the emergency door. It opened, and I shoved him through, sprawling into the snow. I followed him outside. The door swung shut behind me. Mulready tried to scramble to his feet. I kicked him in the stomach. I was wearing my Herman survivor boots, double-insulated with a heavy sole. He gasped. The kick rolled him over onto his back in the snow. He tried to keep rolling. I landed on his chest with both knees. He made a croaking noise.

I said, "I will beat you into whipped cream, Michael, if you don't do just what I say." Then I stood up, yanked him to his feet, got a hold on the back of his collar, and ran him toward my car. He was doubled over with pain, and the wind was knocked out of him and he was easy to move. I shoved him into the front seat, driver's side, put my foot on his backside, and shoved him across to the passenger's side, got in after him, and skidded into reverse. In the rearview mirror I could see three, then four men and the girl from the call counter coming out the emergency exit. I shifted into third and pulled out of the parking lot and past the gate house; the guard gestured at us. I turned right through the parking lot at the Howard Johnson's motel and out onto the Southeast Expressway.

In the rearview mirror all was serene. The snow slanted in across the road steadily. Beside me Mulready was getting his breath back.

"Where you going with me?" he said. His voice was husky with strain.

"Just riding," I said. "I'm going to ask you questions, and when you've answered them all, and I'm happy with what you've said, I'll drop you off somewhere convenient."

"I don't know anything about anything."

"In that case," I said, "I will pull in somewhere and maybe kill you."

"For what, man? We didn't do you no harm. We didn't plan to do you in. We were supposed to scare you and the broad."

"You mean Ms. Wallace, scumbag."

"Huh?"

"Call her Ms. Wallace. Don't call her 'the broad.'"

"Okay, sure, Ms. Wallace. Okay by me. We weren't trying to hurt Ms. Wallace or you, man."

"Who told you to do that?"

"Whaddya mean?"

I shook my head. "You are going to get yourself in very bad trouble," I said. I reached under my coat and brought out my gun and showed it to him. "Smith and Wesson," I said, "thirty-eight caliber, four-inch barrel. Not good for long range, but perfect for shooting a guy sitting next to you."

"Jesus, man, put the piece down. I just didn't understand the question, you know? I mean, What is it you're asking, man? I'll try. You don't need the fucking piece, you know?"

I put the gun back. We were in Milton now; traffic was very thin in the snow. "I said, Who told you to scare us up on the Lynnway that night?"

"My cousin, man—Mingo. He told us about doing it. Said there was a deuce in it for us. Said we could split a deuce for doing it. Mingo, man. You know him?"

"Why did Mingo want you to scare me and Ms. Wallace?"

"I don't know, man, it was just an easy two bills. Swisher says it's a tit. Says he knows how to work it easy. He done time, Swisher. Mingo don't say why, man. He just lays the deuce on us—we ain't asking no questions. A couple hours' drive for that kind of bread, man, we don't even know who you are."

"Then how'd you pick us up?"

"Mingo gave us a picture of the bro—Ms. Wallace. We followed her when you took her out to Marblehead. We hung around till you took her home, and there wasn't much traffic. You know? Then we made our move like he said—Mingo."

"What's Mingo do?"

"You mean for a living?"

"Yeah."

"He works for some rich broad in Belmont."

"Doing what?"

"I don't know. Everything. Drives her around. Carry

stuff when she shops. Errands. That shit. He's got it made, man."

"What's her name?"

"The rich broad?" Mulready shrugged. His breath was back. I had put the gun away. He was talking, which was something he obviously had practiced at. He was beginning to relax a little. "I don't know," he said. "I don't think Mingo ever said."

At Furnace Brook Parkway I went off the expressway, reversed directions, and came back on heading north.

"Where we going now?" Mulready said.

"We're going to go visit Cousin Mingo," I said. "You're going to show me where he lives."

"Oh, fuck me, man. I can't do that. Mingo will fucking kill me."

"But that will be later," I said. "If you don't show me I'll kill you now."

"No, man, you don't know Mingo. He is a bad-ass son of a bitch. I'm telling you now, man, you don't want to fuck with Mingo."

"I told you, Michael. I'm looking for Rachel Wallace. I told you back in the warehouse that I'd break things if I had to. You're one of the things I'll break."

"Well, shit, man, lemme tell you, and then drop me off. Man, I don't want Mingo to know it was me. You don't know what he's fucking like, man."

"What's his real name?" I said.

"Eugene, Eugene Ignatius Mulready."

"We'll check a phonebook," I said.

In Milton I pulled off the expressway and we checked

the listing in an outdoor phonebooth. It didn't list Watertown.

"That's in the West Suburban book," Michael said. "They only got Boston and South Suburban here."

"Observant," I said. "We'll try Information."

"Christ, you think I'm lying? Hey, man, no way. You know? No way I'm going to bullshit you, man, with the piece you're carrying. I mean my old lady didn't raise no stupid kids, you know?"

I put in a dime and dialed Information. "In Watertown," I said. "The number for Eugene I. Mulready—what's the address, Michael?"

He told me. I told the operator.

"The number is eight-nine-nine," she said, "seven-three-seven-oh."

I said thank you and hung up. The dime came back.

"Okay, Michael, you're on your way."

"From here?"

"Yep."

"Man, I got no coat—I'll freeze my ass."

"Call a cab."

"A cab? From here? I ain't got that kind of bread, man."

I took the dime out of the return slot. "Here," I said. "Call your buddy Swisher. Have him come get you."

"What if he ain't home?"

"You're a grown-up person, Michael. You'll figure something out. But I'll tell you one thing—you call and warn Mingo, and you won't grow up any more."

"I ain't going to call Mingo, man. I'd have to tell him I tipped you."

"That's what I figure," I said. I got in my car. Michael

Mulready was standing shivering in his shirt sleeves, his hands in his pants pocket, his shoulders hunched.

"I give you one tip though, pal," he said. "You got a big surprise coming, you think you can fuck around with Mingo like you done with me. Mingo will fucking destroy you."

"Watch," I said and let the clutch out and left him on the sidewalk.

24

WATERTOWN WAS NEXT to Belmont, but only in location. It was mostly working-class and the houses were shabby, often two-family, and packed close together on streets that weren't plowed well. It was slow going now, the snow coming hard and the traffic overcautious and crawling.

Mingo Mulready's house was square, two stories, with a wide front porch. The cedar shingle siding was painted blue. The asbestos shingles on the roof were multi-colored. I parked on the street and walked across.

There were two front entrance doors. The one on the left said Mulready. I rang the bell. Nothing. I waited a minute, rang it again. Then I leaned on it for about two minutes. Mingo wasn't home. I went back to my car. Mingo was probably off working at his soft job, driving the rich woman around Belmont. I turned on the radio and listened to the news at noon. Two things occurred to me. One was that nothing that ever got reported in the news seemed to have anything to do with me, and the other was that it was lunchtime. I drove about ten blocks to the Eastern Lamjun Bakery on Belmont Street and bought a package of fresh Syrian bread, a pound of feta cheese, and a pound of Calamata olives.

The bread was still warm. Then I went across the street to the package store and bought a six-pack of Beck's beer, then I drove back and parked in front of Mingo's house and had lunch, and listened to a small suburban station that played jazz and big-band music. At three I drove down the block to a gas station and filled my gas tank and used the men's room and drove back up to Mingo's and sat some more.

I remembered this kind of work as less boring fifteen years ago when I used to smoke. Probably not so. Probably just seemed that way. At four fifteen Mingo showed up. He was driving a tan Thunderbird with a vinyl roof. He pulled into the driveway beside the house and got out. I got out and walked across the street. We met at the front steps of his home.

I said, "Are you Mingo Mulready?"

He said, "Who wants to know?"

I said, "I say, 'I do,' then you say, 'Who are you?' then I say—"

He said, "What the fuck are you talking about, Jack?"

He was big enough to talk that way, and he must have been used to getting away with it. He was about my height, which made him just under six two, and he was probably twenty-five or thirty pounds heavier, which would have made him 230. He had one of the few honest-to-God boot-camp crew cuts I'd seen in the last eight or ten years. He also had small eyes and a button nose in a doughy face, so that he looked like a mean, palefaced gingerbread man. He was wearing a dark suit and a white shirt and black gloves. He wore no coat.

I said, "Are you Mingo Mulready?"

"I want to know who's asking," he said. "And I want to know pretty quick, or I might stomp your ass."

I was holding my right hand in my left at about belt level. While I was talking I strained the right against the left, so that when I let go with the left, the right snapped up, and the edge of my hand caught Mingo under the nose the way a cocked hammer snaps when you squeeze the trigger. I accelerated it a little on the way up, and the blood spurted from Mingo's nose, and he staggered back about two steps. It was a good shot.

"That's why I wanted to know if you were Mingo," I said. I drove a left hook into the side of his jaw. "Because I didn't want to beat hell out of some innocent bystander." I put a straight right onto Mingo's nose. He fell down. "But you're such a pain in the ass that you need to get the hell beat out of you even if you aren't Mingo Mulready."

He was not a bunny. I'd sucker-punched him and put two more good shots in his face, and he didn't stay down. He came lunging up at me and knocked me back into the snow and scrambled on top of me. I put the heels of both hands under his chin and drove his head back and half-lifted him off me and rolled away. He came after me again, but that extra thirty pounds wasn't helping him. It was mostly fat, and he was already rasping for breath. I moved in, hit him hard twice in the gut, moved out, and hit him twice on that bloody nose. He sagged. I hit him on each side of the jaw. Left jab, right cross, left jab, right cross. He sagged more. His breath wheezed; his arms dropped. He was arm-weary in the first round.

I said, "Are you Mingo Mulready?"

He nodded.

"You sure?" I said. "I heard you were a bad ass."

He nodded again, wheezing for oxygen.

"I guess I heard wrong," I said. "You work for a rich woman in Belmont?"

He stared at me.

"If you want to keep getting your breath back, you answer what I ask. You don't answer, and you'll think what we did before was dancing."

He nodded.

"You do. What's her name?"

"English," he said.

"She tell you to hire your cousin and his pal Swisher to run me off the road in Lynn?"

He said, "You?"

"Yeah, me. Me and Rachel Wallace. Who told you to harass us?"

He looked toward the street. It was empty. The snow was thin and steady, and darkness had come on. He looked toward the house. It was dark.

He said, "I dunno what you mean."

I hit him a good left hook in the throat. He gasped and clutched at his neck.

I said, "Who told you to run Rachel Wallace off the road? Who told you to hire your cousin and his pal? Who gave you the two bills?"

He was having trouble speaking. "English," he croaked.

"The old lady or the son?"

"The son."

"Why?"

He shook his head. I moved my left fist. He backed up. "Swear on my mother," he said. "I don't ask them questions. They pay me good. They treat me decent." He stopped and coughed and spit some blood. "I don't ask no questions. I do what they say, they're important people."

"Okay," I said. "Remember, I know where you live. I may come back and talk with you again. If I have to look for you, it will make me mad."

He didn't say anything. I turned and walked across the street to my car. It was very dark now, and in the snow I couldn't even see the car till I was halfway across the street. I opened the door. The inside light went on. Frank Belson was sitting in the front seat. I got in and closed the door.

"For crissake turn the motor on and get the heater going," he said. "I'm freezing my nuts off."

25

"YOU WANT A beer?" I said. "There's four left in the back seat."

"I don't drink on duty," he said. He took two bottles of Beck's out of the carton. "For crissake, what kind of beer is this? It doesn't even have a twist-off cap."

"There's an opener in the glove compartment," I said.

Belson opened the two beers, gave one to me and took a long pull on the other bottle.

"What you get from Mingo?"

"I thought I was ostracized," I said.

"You know Marty," Belson said. "He gets mad quick, he cools down quick. What you get from Mingo?"

"Haven't you talked to him?"

"We figured you could talk with him harder than we could. We were right. But I thought he'd give you more trouble than he did."

"I suckered him," I said. "That got him off to a bad start."

"Still," Belson said, "he used to be goddamned good."

"Me, too," I said.

"I know that. What'd you get?"

"English set up the hit-and-run on the Lynnway."

"Mingo do it through his cousin?"

"Yeah."

"Cousin tell you that?"

"Yeah. Him and Cody did the work. Mingo gave them a deuce. He got the money from English. I braced Cousin Michael this morning."

"I know," Belson said.

"What the hell is this—practice teaching? You follow me around and observe?"

"I told you we had Cody and Mulready staked out," Belson said. "When you showed up, the detail called in. I told them to let you go. I figured you'd get more than we would because you don't have to sweat brutality charges. They lost you heading out of Sears, but I figured you'd end up here and I came over. Got here about one thirty and been sitting in the next block since. You get anything else?"

"No. But English is looking better and better. You look into those pie-throwers in Cambridge?"

Belson finished the beer and opened another bottle. "Yeah," he said. "There's nothing there. Just a couple of right-wing fruitcakes. They never been in jail. They don't show any connection with English or Mingo Mulready or the Vigilance Committee or anybody else. They go to MIT, for crissake."

"Okay. How about Julie Wells? You talk to her yet?"

Belson held the beer between his knees while he got a half-smoked cigar out of his shirt pocket and lit it and puffed at it. Then he took the cigar out of his mouth, sipped some beer, put the cigar back in, and said around it, "Can't find her. She doesn't seem to have moved or anything, but she's not at her apartment whenever we show up. We're sort of looking for her."

"Good. You think you might sort of find her in a while?"

"If we'd known some things earlier, buddy, we'd have been more likely to have kept an eye on her."

"Know anything about Mingo? You sound like you've known him before."

"Oh, yeah, old Mingo. He's got a good-sized file. Used to work for Joe Broz once. Used to be a bouncer, did some pro wrestling, some loansharking. Been busted for assault, for armed robbery, been picked up on suspicion of murder and released when we couldn't turn a witness that would talk. English employs some sweetheart to drive the old babe around."

I said, "You people going to keep English under surveillance?"

"Surveillance? Christ, you been watching *Police Woman* again? *Surveillance.* Christ."

I said, "You gonna watch him?"

"Yeah. We'll try to keep someone on him. We ain't got all that many bodies, you know?"

"And he's got money and maybe knows a couple city councilmen and a state senator."

"Maybe. It happens. You know Marty. You know me. But you also know how it works. Pressure comes down, we gotta bend. Or get other work, you know?"

"Felt any pressure yet?"

Belson shook his head. "Nope," he said, "not yet." He finished the bottle of beer.

"Belmont cops?"

"They said they could help out a little."

"You got anybody at Julie Wells's apartment?"

"Yeah. And we check in at the agency regular. She ain't there."

I said, "You want a ride to your car?"

He nodded, and I went around the block and dropped him off on the street behind Mingo's house. "You stumble across anything, you might want to give us a buzz," Belson said as he got out.

"Yeah," I said. "I might."

He said, "Thanks for the beer," and closed my door, and I pulled away. It was almost an hour and a half in the snow and the near-motionless rush hour until I got to my apartment. Susan was there.

"I had an Adolescent Development Workshop at B.U. this afternoon, and when I got out it was too bad to drive home, so I left my car in the lot and walked down," she said.

"You missed a golden opportunity," I said.

"For what?"

"To take off all your clothes and make a martini and surprise me at the door."

"I thought of that," Susan said, "but you don't like martinis."

"Oh," I said.

"But I made a fire," she said. "And we could have a drink in front of it."

"Or something," I said. I picked her up and hugged her.

She shook her head. "They were talking about you all day today," she said.

"At the workshop on adolescent development?"

She nodded and smiled her fallen-seraph smile at me. "You exhibit every symptom," she said.

I put her down and we went to the kitchen. "Let us see what there is to eat," I said. "Maybe pulverized rhino horn with a dash of Spanish fly."

"You whip up something, snooks," she said. "I'm going to take a bath. And maybe rinse out the pantyhose in your sink."

"A man's work is never done," I said. I looked in the refrigerator. There was Molson Golden Ale on the bottom shelf. If we were snowbound, at least I had staples on hand. In the vegetable keeper there were some fresh basil leaves and a bunch of parsley I'd bought in Quincy Market. It was a little limp but still serviceable. I opened a Molson. I could hear the water running in the bathroom. I raised the bottle of ale, and said, "Here's looking at you, kid," in a loud voice.

Susan yelled back, "Why don't you make me a gimlet, blue eyes, and I'll drink it when I get out. Ten minutes."

"Okay."

In the freezer was chopped broccoli in a twenty-ounce bag. I took it out. I got out a large blue pot and boiled four quarts of water, and a smaller saucepan with a steamer rack and boiled about a cup of water. While it was coming to a boil I put two garlic cloves in my Cuisinart along with a handful of parsley and a handful of basil and some kosher salt and some oil and a handful of shelled pistachios and I blended them smooth. Susan had given me the Cuisinart for my birthday, and I used it whenever I could. I thought it was kind of a silly toy, but she'd loved giving it to me and

I'd never tell. When the water boiled, I shut off both pots. I could hear Susan sloshing around in the tub. The door was ajar, and I went over and stuck my head in. She lay on her back with her hair pinned up and her naked body glistening in the water.

"Not bad," I said, "for a broad your age."

"I knew you'd peek," she said. "Voyeurism, a typical stage in adolescent development."

"Not bad, actually, for a broad of anyone's age," I said.

"Go make the gimlet now," she said. "I'm getting out."

"Gin or vodka?" I said.

"Gin."

"Animal," I said.

I went back to the kitchen and mixed five parts gin to one part Rose's limejuice in a pitcher and stirred it with ice and poured it into a glass with two icecubes. Susan came into the kitchen as I finished, wearing the half-sleeved silk shaving robe she'd given me last Christmas, which I never wore, but which she did when she came and stayed. It was maroon with black piping and a black belt. When I tried it on, I looked like Bruce Lee. She didn't.

She sat on one of my kitchen stools and sipped her gimlet. Her hair was up and she had no make-up and her face was shiny. She looked fifteen, except for the marks of age and character around her eyes and mouth. They added.

I had another Molson and brought my two pots to a boil again. In the big one I put a pound of spaghetti. In the small one with the steamer rack I put the frozen broccoli. I set the timer for nine minutes.

"Shall we dine before the fire?" I said.

"Certainly."

"Okay," I said. "Put down the booze and take one end of the dining-room table."

We moved it in front of the fire and brought two chairs and set the table while the spaghetti boiled and the broccoli steamed. The bell on the timer rang. I went to the kitchen and drained the broccoli and tried the spaghetti. It needed another minute. While it boiled I ran the Cuisinart another whirl and reblended my oil and spices. Then I tried the pasta. It was done. I drained it, put it back in the pot and tossed it with the spiced oil and broccoli. I put out the pot, the leftover loaves of Syrian bread that I bought for lunch, and a cold bottle of Soave Bolla. Then I held Susan's chair. She sat down. I put another log on the fire, poured a dash of wine in her glass. She sipped it thoughtfully, then nodded at me. I filled her glass and then mine.

"Perhaps madam would permit me to join her," I said.

"Perhaps," she said.

I sipped a little wine.

"And perhaps later on," she said, "we might screw."

I laughed halfway through a swallow of wine and choked and gasped and splattered the wine all over my shirt front.

"Or perhaps not," she said.

"Don't toy with me while I'm drinking," I said, when I was breathing again. "Later on I may take you by force."

"Woo-woo," she said.

I served her some pasta with broccoli and some to myself. Outside it was snowing steadily. There was only one light on in the room; most of the light came from the fire, which was made of applewood and smelled sweet. The glow of the embers behind the steady low flame made the room faintly rosy. We were quiet. The flame hissed softly as it forced the last traces of sap from the logs. I wasn't nearly as sore as I had been. The pasta tasted wonderful. The wine was cold. And Susan made my throat ache. If I could find Rachel Wallace, I might believe in God.

26

THE SUN THAT brief December day rose cheerlessly and invisibly over one hell of a lot of snow in the city of Boston. I looked at the alarm clock. Six AM. It was very still outside, the noise of a normal morning muffled by the snow. I was lying on my right side, my left arm over Susan's bare shoulder. Her hair had come unpinned in the night and was in a wide tangle on the pillow. Her face was toward me and her eyes were closed. She slept with her mouth open slightly, and the smell of wine on her breath fluttered faintly across the pillow. I pushed up on one elbow and looked out the window. The snow was still coming—steadily and at a slant so I knew the wind was driving it. Without opening her eyes, Susan pulled me back down against her and shrugged the covers back up over us. She made a snuggling motion with her body and lay still.

I said, "Would you like an early breakfast, or did you have another plan?"

She pressed her face into the hollow of my shoulder. "My nose is cold," she said in a muffled voice.

"I'm your man," I said. I ran my hand down the line of her body and patted her on the backside. She put her right hand in the small of my back and pressed a little harder against me.

"I had always thought," she said, her face still pressed in my shoulder, "that men of your years had problems of sexual dysfunction."

"Oh, we do," I said. "I used to be twice as randy twenty years ago."

"They must have kept you in a cage," she said. She walked her fingers up my backbone, one vertebra at a time.

"Yeah," I said, "but I could reach through the bars."

"I bet you could," she said, and with her eyes still closed she raised her head and kissed me with her mouth open.

It was nearly eight when I got up and took a shower.

Susan took hers while I made breakfast and built another fire. Then we sat in front of the fire and ate cornbread made with buttermilk, and wild-strawberry jam and drank coffee.

At nine fifteen, with the cornbread gone and the strawberry jam depleted and the *Globe* read and the *Today Show* finished, I called my answering service. Someone had left a telephone number for me to call.

I dialed it, and a woman answered on the first ring. I said, "This is Spenser. I have a message to call this number."

She said, "Spenser, this is Julie Wells."

I said, "Where are you?"

She said, "It doesn't matter. I've got to see you."

I said, "We're in an old Mark Stevens movie."

"I beg your pardon?"

"I want to see you, too," I said. "Where can I meet you?"

"There's a snow emergency, you know."

They never said that in the old Mark Stevens movies. "Name a place," I said. "I'll get there."

"The coffee shop at the Parker House."

"When?"

"Ten thirty."

"See you then."

"I don't want anyone else to know I'm there, Spenser."

"Then you say, 'Make sure you're not followed.' And I say, 'Don't worry. I'll be careful.' "

"Well, I don't. I meant it."

"Okay, kid. I'll be there."

We hung up. Susan was in the bathroom doing make-up. I stuck my head in and said, "I have to go out and work for a while." She was doing something with a long thin pencilish-looking item to the corner of her mouth. She said, "Unh-huh," and kept on doing it.

When Susan concentrates, she concentrates. I put on my white wide-wale corduroy pants, my dark-blue all-wool Pendleton shirt, and my Herman survivors. I put my gun in its hip holster on my belt; I got into my jacket, turned up the fleece collar, pulled on my watch cap, slipped on my gloves, and went forth into the storm.

Except for the snow, which still fell hard, the city was nearly motionless. There was no traffic. The streets were snow-covered, maybe two feet deep, and the snow had drifted in places high enough to bury a parked car. Arlington Street had been partially plowed, and the walking was easier. I turned right on Beacon and headed up the hill, leaning now into the wind and the snow. I pulled my watch cap down over my ears and forehead. It didn't look rakish, but one must compromise occasionally with nature. An enormous yellow bulldozer with an enclosed cab and a plow blade approximately the size of Rhode Island came churning slowly down Beacon Street. There were no people and no dogs, just me and the bulldozer and the snow. When the bulldozer passed, I had to climb over a snowbank to get out of the way of the plow spill, but after it had passed, the walking was much better. I walked up the middle of Beacon Street with the old elegant brick houses on my left and the empty Common on my right. I could see the houses okay, but ten feet past the iron fence the Common disappeared into the haze of snow and strong wind.

At the top of the hill I could see the State House but not the gold dome. Nothing was open. It was downhill from there and a little easier. By the time I got to the Parker House, where Beacon ends at Tremont, I was cold and a little strange with the empty swirling silence in the middle of the city.

There were people hanging around in the lobby of the Parker House and the coffee shop on the Tremont Street side was nearly full. I spotted Julie Wells alone at a table for two by the window looking out at the snow.

She had on a silver ski parka which she'd unzipped but not removed; the hood was thrown back, and the fur trim tangled with the edges of her hair. Underneath the parka she wore a white turtleneck sweater, and with her big gold earrings and her long eyelashes she looked like maybe 1.8 million. Susan was a two million.

I rolled my watch cap back up to rakish and then walked over and sat down across from her. The Parker House used to be Old Boston and kind of an institution. It had fallen on hard times and was now making a comeback, but the coffee shop with the window on Tremont Street was a good place. I unzipped my coat.

"Good morning," I said.

She smiled without much pleasure and said, "I am glad to see you. I really didn't know who else to call."

"I hope you didn't have to walk far," I said. "Even an Olympic walker like myself experienced some moments of discomfort."

Julie said, "There's someone after me."

I said, "I don't blame him."

She said, "There really is. I've seen him outside my apartment. He's followed me to and from work."

"You know the cops have been looking for you."

"About Rachel?"

I nodded. The waitress came, and I ordered coffee and whole-wheat toast. There was a plate with most of an omelet still left on it in front of Julie Wells. The waitress went away.

"I know about the police," she said. "I called the agency, and they said the police had been there, too. But they wouldn't follow me around like that."

I shrugged. "Why not tell the cops about this guy that's following you. If it's one of them, they'll know. If it's not, they can look into it."

She shook her head.

"No cops?"

She shook her head again.

"Why not?"

She poked at the omelet with the tines of her fork, moving a scrap of egg around to the other side of the plate.

"You're not just hiding out from the guy that's following you?" I said.

"No."

"You don't want to talk with the cops either."

She started to cry. Her shoulders shook a little, and her lower lip trembled a little, and some tears formed in her eyes. It was discreet crying though—nothing the other customers would notice.

"I don't know what to do," she said. "I don't want to be involved in all of this. I want people to leave me alone."

"You got any thoughts on where Rachel might be?" I said.

She blew her nose in a pink Kleenex and inhaled shakily. "What shall I do?" she said to me. "I don't know anyone else to ask."

"You know where Rachel is?"

"No, of course not. How would I? We were friends, lovers if you'd rather, but we weren't in love or anything. And if people—"

"You don't want people to know that you're a lesbian."

She made a little shiver. "God, I hate the word. It's so . . . clinical, like classifying an odd plant."

"But you still don't want it known?"

"Well, I'm not ashamed. You put it so baldly. I have made a life choice that's not like yours, or some others, and I have no reason to be ashamed. It's as natural as anyone else."

"So why not talk with the cops? Don't you want to find Rachel Wallace?"

She clasped her hands together and pressed the knuckles against her mouth. Tears formed again. "Oh, God, poor Rachel. Do you think she's alive?"

The waitress brought my toast and coffee.

When she left, I said, "I don't have any way to know. I have to assume she is, because to assume she isn't leaves me nothing to do."

"And you're looking for her?"

"I'm looking for her."

"If I knew anything that would help, I'd say so. But what good will it do Rachel to have my name smeared in the papers? To have the people at the model agency—"

"I don't know what good," I said. "I don't know what you know. I don't know why someone is following you, or was—I assume you've lost him."

She nodded. "I got away from him on the subway."

"So who would he be? Why would he follow you? It's an awful big coincidence that Rachel is taken and then someone follows you."

"I don't know, I don't know anything. What if they want to kidnap me? I don't know what to do." She stared out the window at the empty snow-covered street.

"Why not stay with your mother and brother?" I said.

She looked back at me slowly. I ate a triangle of toast.

"What do you know about my mother and brother?"

"I know their names and I know their politics and I know their attitude toward Rachel Wallace, and I can guess their attitude toward you if they knew that you and Rachel were lovers."

"Have you been . . . did you . . . you don't have the right to . . ."

"I haven't mentioned you to them. I did mention you to the cops, but only when I had to, quite recently"

"Why did you have to?"

"Because I'm looking for Rachel, and I'll do anything

I have to to find her. When I figured out that you were Lawrence English's sister, I thought it might be a clue. It might help them find her. They're looking, too."

"You think my brother—"

"I think he's in this somewhere. His chauffeur hired two guys to run me and Rachel off the road one night in Lynn. Your brother organized a picket line when she spoke in Belmont. Your brother has said she's an ungodly corruption or some such. And he's the head of an organization of Ritz crackers that would be capable of such things."

"I didn't used to know I was gay," she said. "I just thought I was not very affectionate. I got married. I felt guilty about being cold. I even did therapy. It didn't work. I was not a loving person. We were divorced. He said I was like a wax apple. I looked wonderful, but there was nothing inside—no nourishment. I went to a support group meeting for people recently divorced, and I met a woman and cared for her, and we developed a relationship, and I found out I wasn't empty. I could love. I could feel passion. It was maybe the moment in my life. We made love and I felt. I"—she looked out the window again, and I ate another piece of toast—"I reached orgasm. It was as if, as if . . . I don't know what it was as if."

"As if a guilty verdict had been overturned."

She nodded. "Yes. Yes. I wasn't bad. I wasn't cold. I had been trying to love the wrong things."

"But Mom and brother?"

"You've met them?"

"Brother," I said. "Not yet Momma."

"They could never understand. They could never accept it. It would be just the worst thing that could be for them. I wish for them—maybe for me, too—I wish it could have been different, but it can't, and it's better to be what I am than to be failing at what I am not. But they mustn't ever know. That's why I can't go to the police. I can't let them know. I don't mind the rest of the world. It's them. They can't know. I don't know what they would do."

"Maybe they'd kidnap Rachel," I said.

27

THE WAITRESS SAID, "May I get you anything else?"

I shook my head, so did Julie. The waitress put the check down, near me, and I put a ten down on top of it.

Julie said, "They wouldn't. They couldn't do that. They wouldn't know what to do."

"They could hire a consultant. Their chauffeur has done time. Name's Mingo Mulready, believe it or not, and he would know what to do."

"But they don't know."

"Maybe they don't. Or maybe the guy that was following you around was your brother's. You haven't been living at home."

"Spenser, I'm thirty years old."

"Get along with the family?"

"No. They didn't approve of my marriage. They didn't approve of my divorce. They hated me going to Goucher. They hate me being a model. I couldn't live with them."

"They worry about you?"

She shrugged. Now that she was thinking, she wasn't crying, and her face looked more coherent. "I suppose they did," she said. "Lawrence likes to play father and man of the house, and Mother lets him. I guess they think I'm dissolute and weak and uncommitted—that kind of thing."

"Why would they have a thug like Mulready driving them around?"

Julie shrugged her shoulders. "Lawrence is all caught up in his Vigilance Committee. He gets into situations, I guess, where he feels he needs a bodyguard. I assume this Mulready is someone who would do that."

"Not as well as he used to," I said.

The waitress picked up my ten and brought back some change on a saucer.

"If they did take Rachel," I said, "where would they keep her?"

"I don't know."

"Sure you do. If you were your brother and you had kidnaped Rachel Wallace, where would you keep her?"

"Oh, for God's sake, Spenser . . ."

"Think," I said. "Think about it. Humor me."

"This is ridiculous."

"I walked a half-mile through a blizzard because you asked me to," I said. "I didn't say it was ridiculous."

She nodded. "The house," she said.

The waitress came back and said, "Can I get you anything else?"

I shook my head. "We better vacate," I said to Julie, "before she gets ugly."

Julie nodded. We left the coffee shop and found an overstuffed loveseat in the lobby.

"Where in the house?" I said.

"Have you seen it?"

"Yeah. I was out there a few days ago."

"Well, you know how big it is. There's probably twenty rooms. There's a great big cellar. There's the chauffeur's quarters over the garage and extra rooms in the attic."

"Wouldn't the servants notice?"

"They wouldn't have to. The cook never leaves the kitchen, and the maid would have no reason to go into some parts of the house. We had only the cook and the maid when I was there."

"And of course old Mingo."

"They hired him after I left. I don't know him."

"Tell you what," I said. "We'll go back to my place. It's just over on Marlborough Street, and we'll draw a map of your brother's house."

"It's my mother's," Julie said.

"Whoever," I said. "We'll make a map, and later on I'll go take a look."

"How will you do that?"

"First the map. Then the B-and-E plans. Come on."

"I don't know if I can make a map."

"Sure you can. I'll help and we'll talk. You'll remember."

"And we're going to your apartment?"

"Yes. It's quite safe. I have a woman staying with me who'll see that I don't molest you. And on the walk down we'll be too bundled up."

"I didn't mean that."

"Okay, let's go."

We pushed out into the snow again. It seemed to be lessening, but the wind was whipping it around so much it was hard to tell. A half-block up Beacon Street Julie took my arm, and she hung on all the way up over the hill and down to Marlborough. Other than two huge yellow pieces of snow equipment that clunked and waddled through the snow, we were all that moved.

When we got to my apartment, Susan was on the couch by the fire reading a book by Robert Coles. She wore a pair of jeans she'd left there two weeks ago and one of my gray T-shirts with the size, XL, printed in red letters on the front. It hung almost to her knees.

I introduced them and took Julie's coat and hung it in the hall closet. As I went by the bathroom, I noticed Susan's lingerie hanging on the shower rod to dry. It made me speculate about what was under the jeans, but I put it from me. I was working. I got a pad of lined yellow paper, legal size, from a drawer in the kitchen next to the phone and a small translucent plastic artist's triangle and a black ballpoint pen, and Julie and I sat at the counter in my kitchen for three hours and diagrammed her mother's house not only the rooms, but what was in them.

"I haven't been there in a year," she said at one point.

"I know, but people don't usually rearrange the big pieces. The beds and sofas and stuff are usually where they've always been."

We made an overall diagram of the house and then did each room on a separate sheet. I numbered all the rooms and keyed them to the separate sheets.

"Why do you want to know all this? Furniture and everything?"

"It's good to know what you can. I'm not sure even what I'm up to. I'm just gathering information. There's so much that I can't know, and so many things I can't predict, that I like to get everything I can in order so when the unpredictable stuff comes along I can concentrate on that."

Susan made a large plate of ham sandwiches while we finished up our maps and we had them with coffee in front of the fire.

"You make a good fire for a broad," I said to Susan.

"It's easy," Susan said, "I rubbed two dry sexists together."

"This is a wonderful sandwich," Julie said to Susan.

"Yes. Mr. Macho here gets the ham from someplace out in eastern New York State."

"Millerton," I said. "Cured with salt and molasses. Hickory-smoked, no nitrates."

Julie looked at Susan. "Ah, what about that other matter?"

"The shadow?" I said.

She nodded.

"You can go home and let him spot you, and then I'll take him off your back."

"Home?"

"Sure. Once he lost you, if he's really intent on staying with you, he'll go and wait outside your home until you show up. What else can he do?"

"I guess nothing. He wouldn't be there today, I wouldn't think."

"Unless he was there yesterday," Susan said. "The governor's been on TV. No cars allowed on the highway. No buses are running. No trains. Nothing coming into the city."

"I don't want to go home," Julie said.

"Or you can stay hiding out for a while, but I'd like to know where to get you."

She shook her head.

"Look, Julie," I said. "You got choices, but they are not limitless. You are part of whatever happened to Rachel Wallace. I don't know what part, but I'm not going to let go of you. I don't have that much else. I need to be able to find you."

She looked at me and at Susan, who was sipping her coffee from a big brown mug, holding it in both hands with her nose half-buried in the cup and her eyes on the fire. Julie nodded her head three times.

"Okay," she said. "I'm in an apartment at one sixty-four Tremont. One of the girls at the agency is in Chicago, and she let me stay while she's away. Fifth floor."

"I'll walk you over," I said.

28

THE DAY AFTER the big blizzard was beautiful, the way it always is. The sun is shining its ass off, and the snow is still white, and no traffic is out, and people and dogs are walking everywhere and being friendly during shared duress.

Susan and I walked out to Boylston and up toward Mass. Ave. She had bought a funky-looking old raccoon coat with padded shoulders when we'd gone antiquing in New Hampshire in November, and she was wearing it with big furry boots and a woolen hat with a big pom-pom. She looked like a cross between Annette Funicello and Joan Crawford.

We'd been living together for two and a half days, and if I had known where Rachel Wallace was, I would have been having a very nice time. But I didn't know where Rachel Wallace was, and what was worse, I had a suspicion where she might be, and I couldn't get there. I had called

Quirk and told him what I knew. He couldn't move against a man of English's clout without some probable cause, and we agreed I had none. I told him I didn't know where Julie Wells was staying. He didn't believe me, but the pressure of the snow emergency was distracting the whole department, and no one came over with a thumbscrew to interrogate me.

So Susan and I walked up Boylston Street to see if there was a store open where she could buy some underclothes and maybe a shirt or two, and I walked with her in a profound funk. All traffic was banned from all highways. No trains were moving.

Susan bought some very flossy-looking lingerie at Saks, and a pair of Levi's and two blouses. We were back out on Boylston when she said, "Want to go home and model the undies?"

"I don't think they'd fit me," I said.

"I didn't mean you," she said.

I said, "God damn it, I'll walk out there."

"Where?"

"I'll walk out to Belmont."

"Just to avoid modeling the undies?"

I shook my head. "It's what? Twelve, fifteen miles? Walk about three miles an hour. I'll be there in four or five hours."

"You're sure she's there?"

"No. But she might be, and if she is, it's partly my fault. I have to look."

"It's a lot of other people's fault much more than yours. Especially the people who took her."

"I know, but if I'd been with her, they wouldn't have taken her."

Susan nodded.

"Why not call the Belmont Police?" she said.

"Same as with Quirk. They can't just charge in there. They have to have a warrant. And there has to be some reasonable suspicion, and I don't have anything to give them. And . . . I don't know. They might screw it up."

"Which means that you want to do it yourself."

"Maybe."

"Even if it endangers her?"

"I don't want to endanger her. I trust me more than I trust anyone else. Her life is on the line here. I want me to be the one who's in charge."

"And because you have to even up with the people that took her," Susan said, "you're willing to go after her alone and risk the whole thing, including both your lives, because your honor has been tarnished, or you think it has."

I shook my head. "I don't want some Belmont cop in charge of this whose last bust was two ninth-graders with an ounce of Acapulco gold."

"And Quirk or Frank Belson can't go because they don't have jurisdiction, and they don't have a warrant and all of the above?"

I nodded.

We turned the corner onto Arlington and walked along in the middle of the bright street, like a scene from Currier and Ives.

"Why don't you find Hawk and have him go with you?"

I shook my head.

"Why not?"

"I'm going alone."

"I thought you would. What if something happens to you?"

"Like what?"

"Like suppose you sneak in there and someone shoots you. If you're right, you are dealing with people capable of that."

"Then you tell Quirk everything you know. And tell Hawk to find Rachel Wallace for me."

"I don't even know how to get in touch with Hawk. Do I call that health club on the waterfront?"

"If something happens to me, Hawk will show up and see if you need anything."

We were on the corner of Marlborough Street. Susan stopped and looked at me. "You know that so certainly?"

"Yes."

She shook her head and kept shaking it. "You people are like members of a religion or a cult. You have little rituals and patterns you observe that nobody else understands."

"What people?"

"People like you. Hawk, Quirk, that state policeman you met when the boy was kidnaped."

"Healy."

"Yes, Healy. The little trainer at the Harbor Health Club. All of you. You're as complexly programmed as male wildebeests, and you have no common sense at all."

"Wildebeests?" I said.

"Or Siamese fighting fish."

"I prefer to think *lion, panther* maybe."

We walked to my apartment. "I suppose," Susan said, "we could settle for ox. Not as strong but nearly as smart."

Susan went to the apartment. I went to the basement and got some more firewood from the storage area and carried an armful up the back stairs. It was early afternoon. We had lunch. We watched the news. The travel ban was still with us.

"At least wait until morning," Susan said. "Get an early start."

"And until then?"

"We can read by the fire."

"When that gets boring, I was thinking we could make shadow pictures on the wall. Ever see my rooster?"

Susan said, "I've never heard it called that." I put my arm around her shoulder and squeezed her against me and we began to giggle. We spent the rest of the day before the fire on the couch. Mostly we read.

29

BY SEVEN THIRTY the next morning I was on the road. I had a flashlight in my hip pocket, a short prying tool stuck in my belt, my packet of floor plans in my shirt pocket, and my usual jackknife and gun. Susan kissed me goodbye without getting up, and I left without hearing any more wildebeest remarks. I walked up Marlborough to the Mass. Ave. Bridge along a quiet and narrow lane, one plow-blade wide, with the snow head-high on either side of me. Below the bridge the Charles was frozen and solid white. No sign of the river. Memorial Drive had one lane cleared in either direction, and I turned west. I had learned to walk some years ago at government expense when I had walked from Pusan to the Yalu River and then back. I moved right along. After the first mile or so I had a nice rhythm and even felt just a trickle of sweat along the line of my backbone.

It was shorter than I thought. I was on Trapelo Road in

Belmont by ten forty-five. By eleven I was standing two houses away from the English place, across the street. Now if I found Rachel Wallace, I wouldn't have to walk back. The cops would drive me. Maybe.

The house was three stories high. Across the front was a wide veranda. A long wing came off the back, and at the end of the wing there was a carriage house with a little pointed cupola on top. Mingo probably parked the family Caddies in the carriage house. There was a back door, which led through a back hall into the kitchen, according to Julie. Off the back hall there were back stairs. The veranda turned one corner and ran back along the short side of the house, the one without the wing. Big french doors opened out onto the library, where I'd talked with English before. The yard wasn't as big as you'd expect with a house like that. Last century when they'd built the house there was plenty of land, so no one had wanted it. Now there wasn't and they did. The neighbor's house was maybe fifty feet away on one side, a street was ten feet away on the other, and the backyard was maybe a hundred feet deep. A chain-link fence surrounded the property, except in front, where there was a stone wall, broken by the driveway. There was no sign of the driveway now and very little of the fence in the high snow. It took me nearly two and a half hours of clambering about through snowbanks and side streets to get all of the layout of the grounds and to look at the house from all sides. When I got through, I was sweaty underneath my jacket, and the shoulder rig I was wearing chafed under my left arm. I figured it was better than walking ten miles with the gun jiggling in a hip holster.

There were people out now, shoveling and walking to the store for supplies, and a lot of laughter and neighborly hellos and a kind of siege mentality that made everyone your buddy. I studied the house. The shutters on the top-floor windows were closed, all of them, on the left side and in front. I strolled around the corner and up the side street to the right of the house. The top-floor shutters were closed there, too. I went on down the road till I could see the back shutters.

I knew where I'd look first if I ever got in there. That was the only detail to work out. Julie had told me there was a burglar alarm, and that her mother had always set it before she went to bed. Going in before Mom went to bed would seem to be the answer to that. It would help if I knew who was in there. Mingo, probably. I saw what looked like his tan Thunderbird barely showing through a snowdrift back by the carriage house. There'd be a maid or two probably, and Momma and Lawrence. Whoever was in there when the storm came would be in there now. There were no tracks, no sign of shoveling, just the smooth white sea of snow out of which the old Victorian house rose like a nineteenth-century ship.

I thought about getting in. Trying the old I'm-from-the-power-company trick. But the odds were bad. English knew me, Mingo knew me. At least one of the maids knew me. If I got caught and they got wise, things would be worse. They might kill Rachel. They might kill me, if they could. And that would leave Rachel with no one looking for her the way I was looking for her. Hawk would find her eventually, but he wouldn't have my motivation. Hawk's way would be prompt though. Maybe he'd find her quicker. He'd hold English out a twenty-story window till English said where Rachel was.

I thought about that. It wasn't a bad way. The question

was, How many people would I have to go through to hang English out the window? There were probably at least five people in there—Mingo, English, Momma, and two maids—but the whole Vigilance Committee could be in there sharpening their pikes for all I knew.

It was two o'clock. Nothing was happening. People like English wouldn't have to come out till April. They'd have food in the pantry and booze in the cellar and fuel in the tank and nothing to make winter inconvenient. Did they have a hostage in the attic? Why hadn't there been some kind of communication? Why no more ransom notes or threats about canceling the books or anything? Had they been snowed out? I didn't know any of the answers to any of the questions, and I could only think of one way to find out.

At two fifteen I waded through the snow, sometimes waist-deep, and floundered up to the front door and rang the bell. If they knew me, they knew me. I'd deal with that if it happened. A maid answered.

I said, "Mr. English, please."

She said, "Who may I say is calling?"

I said, "Joseph E. McCarthy."

She said, "Just a moment, please," and started to close the door.

I said, "Wait a minute. It's cold, and we've had a blizzard. Couldn't I wait in the front hall?"

And she hesitated and I smiled at her disarmingly but a bit superior, and she nodded and said, "Of course, sir. I'm sorry. Come in."

I went in. She closed the door behind me and went off down the corridor and through a door and closed it behind her. I went up the front stairs as quietly as I could. There was a landing and then a short left turn, then three steps to the upstairs hall. Actually there were two upstairs halls. One ran from front to back and the other, like the cross of a capital **T**, ran the width of the house and led into the wing hall.

I had the general layout in my head. I'd spent most of my time in front of yesterday's fire looking at Julie's diagrams. The stairway to the attic was down the hall in a small back bedroom. The house was quiet. Faintly somewhere I could hear television. There was a smell of violet sachet and mothballs in the small bedroom. The door to the stairs was where it should have been. It was a green wooden door made of narrow vertical boards with a small bead along one edge. It was closed. There was a padlock on it.

Behind me I heard no hue and cry. The maid would be returning now to say that Mr. English didn't know a Joseph E. McCarthy, or that the one he knew wasn't likely to be calling here. I took my small pry bar from my belt. The padlock hasp wasn't very new, and neither was the door. The maid would look and not see me and be puzzled and would look outside and perhaps around downstairs a little before she reported to English that Mr. McCarthy had left. I wedged the blade of the pry bar under the hasp and pulled the whole thing out of the wood, screws and all. It probably wasn't much louder than the clap of Creation. It just seemed so because I was tense. The door opened in, and the stairs went up a right angle, very steep, very narrow treads and high risers. I closed the door and went up the stairs with hand and feet touching like a hungry monkey. Upstairs the attic was pitch-black. I got out my flashlight and snapped it on and held it in my teeth to keep my hands free. I had the pry bar in my right hand.

The attic was rough and unfinished except for what appeared to be two rooms, one at each gabled end. All the windows had plywood over them. I took one quick look and noticed the plywood was screwed in, not nailed. Someone had wanted it to be hard to remove. I tried one door at the near end of the attic. It was locked. I went and tried the other. It opened, and I went in holding the pry bar like a weapon. Except for an old metal frame bed and a big steamer trunk and three cardboard boxes it was empty. The windows were covered with plywood.

If Rachel was up here, she was back in the other room at the gable end. And she was here—I could feel her. I could feel my insides clench with the certainty that she was behind that other door. I went back to it. There was a padlock, this one new, with a new hasp. I listened. No sound from the room. Downstairs I could hear footsteps. I rammed the pry bar in under the hasp and wrenched the thing loose. The adrenaline was pumping, and I popped the whole thing off and ten feet across the attic floor with one lunge. There was saliva on my chin from holding the flashlight. I took the light in my hand and shoved into the room. It stunk. I swept the flashlight around. On an iron-frame bed with a gray blanket around her, half-raised, was Rachel Wallace, and she looked just awful. Her hair was a mess, and she had no make-up, and her eyes were swollen. I reversed the flashlight and shone it on my face.

"It's Spenser," I said.

"Oh, my God," she said. Her voice was hoarse.

The lights went on suddenly. There must have been a

downstairs switch, and I'd missed it. The whole attic was bright. I snicked off the flashlight and put it in my pocket and took out my gun and said, "Get under the bed."

Rachel rolled onto the floor and under the bed. Her feet were bare. I heard footsteps coming up the stairs, and then they stopped. They'd spotted the ruptured door. It sounded like three sets of footsteps. I looked up. The light in this room came from a bare bulb that hung from a zinc fixture in the ceiling. I reached up with the pry bar and smashed the bulb. The room was dark except for the light from beyond the door.

Outside, a woman's voice said, "Who is in there?" It was an old voice but not quavery and not weak. I didn't say anything. Rachel made no sound.

The voice said, "You are in trespass in there. I want you out. There are two armed men out here. You have no chance."

I got down on the floor and snaked along toward the door.

In the light at the head of the stairs was Mingo with a double-barreled shotgun and English with an automatic pistol. Between them and slightly forward was a woman who looked like a man, and an ugly, mean man at that. She was maybe five eight and heavy, with a square massive face and short gray hair. Her eyebrows came straight across with almost no arch and met over the bridge of her nose. They were black.

"Give yourself up," she said. There was no uncertainty in her voice and certainly no fear. She was used to people doing what she said.

From the dark I said, "It's over, Momma. People know I'm here. They know I was looking for Rachel Wallace. And I found her. Throw down the weapons, and I'll bring her out and take her home. Then I'll call the cops. You'll have that much time to run."

"Run?" Momma said. "We want you out of there and we'll have you out now. You and that atrocious queer." Mingo had brought the shotgun to the ready and was looking into the room.

I said "Last chance," and rolled right, over once, and came up with my gun raised and steadied with my left hand. Mingo fired one barrel toward where I had been, and I shot him under the right eye. He fell backwards down the stairs. English began to shoot into the room—vaguely, I guess in the direction of my muzzle flash, but panicky and without much time to aim. He squeezed off four rounds into the dark room and I shot him, twice, carefully. One bullet caught him in the forehead and the second in the throat. He made no sound and fell forward. He was probably dead before he landed. I saw Momma start to bend, and I thought she might keel over, but then I realized she was going for the gun, and I lunged to my feet and jumped three jumps and kicked it away from her, and yanked her to her feet by the back of her collar. There was a little bubble of saliva at the corner of her mouth, and she began to gouge at my eyes with her fingers. I held her at arm's length—my arms were longer than hers—and looked down at Mingo in a tangle at the foot of the stairs. He was dead. He had the look. You see it enough, you know.

I said, "Mrs. English, they're dead. Both of them. Your son is dead."

She spat at me and dug her fingernails into my wrist and tried to bite my arm. I said, "Mrs. English, I'm going to hit you."

She bit my arm. It didn't hurt, because she was trying to

bite through my coat, but it made me mad. I put my gun away, and I slapped her hard across the face. She began to scream at me. No words, just scream and claw and bite and I hit her with my right fist, hard. She fell down and began to snivel, her face buried in her son's dead back. I picked up English's gun and stuck it in my pocket and went down the stairs and got Mingo's shotgun and jacked the remaining shell out and put that in my pocket and went back up the stairs.

Rachel was standing in the doorway of the room, looking at the carnage and squinting in the light. She had the gray blanket wrapped around her and held with both hands closed at the neck.

I walked over to her and said, "Okay, Jane Eyre, I got you."

Tears began to run down her face, and I put my arms around her, and she cried. And I cried. In between crying I said, "I got you. I got you."

She didn't say anything.

30

THE FIRST COPS to show were cruiser people—three cars' worth despite the snow emergency—and one of them was Foley, the young cop with the ribbons and the wise-guy face. They came up the attic stairs with guns drawn, directed by the frightened maid who'd called them. He was first. He knew who Rachel was the first look he took.

"Son of a bitch," he said. "You found her."

His partner with the belly squatted down beside English and felt his neck. Then he and another prowlie half-lifted, half-helped Momma English off her son's body. While the prowlie held her, the pot-bellied cop got down on his hands and knees and listened to English's chest. He looked at the young cop and shook his head.

"Gonzo," he said. "So's the horse at the bottom." He nodded at Mingo, still sprawled at the foot of the attic stairs. They must have had to climb over him. "Two in the head," he said. He stood up and looked at me. I still had my arms around Rachel. "What the hell you crying for?" he said. "Think how these guys feel."

Foley spun around. "Shut up," he said. "I know why he's crying. You don't. Close your fucking mouth up."

The older cop shook his head and didn't say anything.

Foley said to me, "You ace these two guys?"

I nodded.

Foley said, "Chief will want to talk with you about all this. Her, too."

"Not now," I said, "now I'm taking her home."

Foley looked at me for maybe thirty seconds. "Yeah," he said. "Take her out of here."

The cop with the belly said, "For crissake, the chief will fry our ass. This clown blasts two guys, one of them Lawrence English, and he walks while we stand around. Foley, we got two stiffs here."

I said to Foley, "I need a ride."

He nodded. "Come on."

His partner said, "Foley, are you fucking crazy?"

Foley put his face close to the older cop's face. "Benny," he said, "you're okay. You're not a bad cop. But you don't know how to act, and you're too old to learn."

"Chief will have your badge for this and mine for letting you do it."

Foley said, "Ain't your fault, Benny. You couldn't stop me."

Mom English said, "If you let that murderer escape and allow that corrupt degenerate to go with him, I'll have every one of your badges."

There were four other cops besides Foley and Benny. One of them had gone downstairs to call in. One was supporting Mrs. English. The other two stood uncertainly. One of them had his gun out, although it hung at his side and he'd probably forgotten he had it in his hand.

"They murdered my son," she said. Her voice was flat and heavy. "She has vomited filth and corruption long enough. She has to be stopped. We would have stopped her if he hadn't interfered. And you must. She is a putrefaction, a cancerous foul sore." The voice stayed flat but a trickle of saliva came from the left corner of her mouth. She breathed heavily through her nose. "She has debauched and destroyed innocent women and lured them into unspeakable acts." Her nose began to run a little.

I said, "Foley, we're going."

He nodded and pushed past Benny. We followed. Rachel still had the blanket around her.

Momma shrieked at us, "She stole my daughter."

One of the other cops said, "Jesus Christ, Fole."

Foley looked at him, and his eyes were hot. Then he went down the attic stairs, and Rachel and I went with him. In the front hall on the first floor the two maids stood, silent and fidgety. The cop on the phone was talking to someone at headquarters and as we went past he glanced up and widened his eyes.

"Where the hell you going?" he said.

Foley shook his head.

"Chief says he's on his way, Fole."

We kept going. On the porch I picked Rachel up—she was still in her bare feet—and carried her through the floundering waist-deep snow. The cruisers were there in front with the blue lights rotating.

Foley said, "First one."

We got in—Foley in front, me and Rachel in back. He hit the siren, and we pulled out.

"Where?" Foley said.

"Boston," I said. "Marlborough Street, Arlington Street end."

Foley left the siren wailing all the way, and with no traffic but cops and plows we made it in fifteen minutes. He pulled into Marlborough Street from Arlington and went up it the wrong way two doors to my apartment.

"You ain't here when we want you," Foley said, "and I'll be working next week in a carwash."

I got out with Rachel. I had been holding her all the way.

I looked at Foley and nodded once.

"Yeah," he said.

He spun the wheels pulling away, slammed the car into snowbanks on both sides of the street making a U-turn and spun the wheels some more as he skidded out into Arlington.

I carried Rachel up to my front door and leaned on my bell till Susan said, "Who is it?" over the intercom.

I said, "Me," never at a loss for repartee.

She buzzed and I pushed and in we went. I called the elevator with my elbow and punched my floor with the same elbow and banged on my door with the toe of my boot. Susan opened it. She saw Rachel.

"Oh," she said. "Isn't that good!"

We went in and I put Rachel down on the couch.

I said, "Would you like a drink?"

She said, "Yes, very much."

"Bourbon, okay?"

"Yes, on the rocks, please."

She still had her gray blanket tightly wrapped around her. I went out in the kitchen and got a bottle of Wild Turkey and three glasses and a bucket of ice and came back out. I poured each of us a drink. Susan had kept the fire going and it went well with the Wild Turkey. Each of us drank.

"You need a doctor?" I said.

"No," she said. "I don't think so. I was not abused in that sense."

"Would you like to talk about it?" Susan said.

"Yes," Rachel said, "I think I would. I shall talk about it and probably write about it. But right now I should very much like to bathe and put on clean clothes, and then perhaps eat something." She drank some bourbon. "I've not," she said, "been eating particularly well lately." She smiled slightly.

"Sure," I said. "Spenser's the name, cooking's the game."

I started to get up. "No," she said. "Stay here a minute, both of you, while I finish this drink."

And so we sat—me and Rachel on the couch, Susan in the wing chair—and sipped the bourbon and looked at the fire. There was no traffic noise and it was quiet except for the hiss of the fire and the tick of the old steeple clock with wooden works that my father had given me years ago.

Rachel finished her drink. "I would like another," she said, "to take into the bath with me."

I mixed it for her.

She said, "Thank you."

Susan said, "If you want to give me your old clothes, I can put them through the wash for you. Lancelot here has all the latest conveniences."

Rachel shook her head. "No," she said. "I haven't any clothes. They took them. I have only the blanket."

Susan said, "Well, I've got some things you can wear."

Rachel smiled. "Thank you," she said.

Susan showed Rachel to the bathroom door. "There are clean towels," Susan said. "While he was out I was being domestic."

Rachel went in and closed the door. I heard the water begin to run in the tub. Susan walked over to me on the couch.

"How are you?" she said.

"Okay," I said.

"Was it bad?"

"Yeah," I said.

"Was it English?"

I nodded. She rubbed my head—the way you tousle a dog.

"What was that old song?" she said. " 'Joltin' Joe DiMaggio, we want you on our side.' "

"Yeah, except around here we used to sing, 'Who's better than his brother Joe? Dominic DiMaggio.' "

She rubbed my head again, "Well, anyway," she said. "I want *you* on my side, cutie."

"You're just saying that," I said, "because DiMaggio's not around."

"That's true," she said.

31

WHILE RACHEL WAS in the bath I made red beans and rice. Susan put out the rest of the cornbread and I chopped green peppers and scallions. When Rachel finally came to dinner, she had put on some of Susan's make-up and a pair of Susan's jeans and a sweatshirt of mine that was considerably big. The sleeves were rolled up and made a bulky ring around her arms above the elbow. Her hair had been washed and blown dry and looked very straight.

I said, "You want some more bourbon?"

She said yes.

I gave her some more, with ice, and she sat at the table in the dining area and sipped it. I served the beans and rice with the chopped vegetables and some canned chopped tomato on top and put out a dish of grated cheddar cheese. Susan and I drank beer with the meal. Rachel stayed with the bourbon. Like the martinis she'd been drinking when we met first, the bourbon seemed to have no effect.

There was very little talk for the first few minutes. Rachel ate rapidly. When she had nearly finished, she said, "Julie is that woman's daughter, did you know that?"

"Yes," I said.

"They took me because of her, you know."

"I thought they might have."

"They wanted to punish me for corrupting their girl child. They wanted to separate us. They wanted to be sure no one would ever see Julie with me. The idea that her daughter could be a lesbian was more than she could think. I think she thought that if I weren't there, Julie would revert to her normal self."

She said *normal* with a lot of bite in it.

"It wasn't anything to do with your books?" Susan said.

"Maybe it was, too," Rachel said. "Especially the man. I think he was more comfortable with the kidnaping if it was for a cause. He called it a political act."

"And what did they plan to do with you?" I said.

"I don't know. I don't think they knew. I think the one that actually took me, the big one that works for them . . ."

"Mingo," I said. "Mingo Mulready."

"I think he wanted to kill me."

"Sure," I said. "You'd make a damaging witness if you survived."

Rachel nodded. "And they didn't conceal their identities. I saw them all, and they told me they were Julie's people."

"Did they treat you badly?" Susan said.

Rachel looked down at her plate. It was empty.

I said, "Would you like more?"

She shook her head. "No. It's very good, but I'm full, thank you."

"More bourbon?" I said.

"You know, that's the thing you've said to me most, since I got here? You must have great faith in its restorative powers."

"It's a way of being solicitous," I said.

"I know," Rachel said. "And yes, I'll have another. I, too, have great faith in its restorative powers."

I got her the bourbon.

"I wonder why they didn't kill me," she said. "I was afraid they would. I'd lie up there in the dark, and each time they came I'd wonder if they had come to kill me."

"Probably didn't have the balls," I said. "Probably would have had to find a way to maneuver themselves into having Mingo do it."

"Like what?" Rachel said.

"Oh, get up some kind of ultimatum and present it to the cops. An ultimatum that couldn't be met. Then they could say it wasn't their fault. They'd been left no choice, and they'd had to do it to stop your poison because the officials were duped by the Antichrist, or the commies, or Gore Vidal, or whoever."

"The mother would have wanted to most," Rachel said. She looked at Susan. "They didn't mistreat me in the sense of torture or anything. I wasn't tied up or beaten. But the mother wanted to humiliate me. And the son. Julie's brother."

"Lawrence," I said.

"Yes, Lawrence." She shivered.

"What did Lawrence do?" Susan said. Her voice was quite soft.

"He used to come up with my food and sit beside me on the bed and ask me about my relations with Julie. He wanted explicit detail. And he would touch me."

I said, "Jesus Christ."

"I think he got excited by the talk of my lovemaking with Julie. And he would say in his position he rarely had the opportunity to be with a woman, how he had to be careful, that he was in an exposed position and couldn't risk being compromised by a woman. And then he would touch me." She stopped.

Susan said, very quietly, "Did he rape you?"

"Not in the traditional sense," Rachel said. "He—" She paused, looking for the right way to say it. "He couldn't in the traditional sense. He seemed unable to erect."

"His mom probably told him not to," I said.

Susan frowned at me a little.

"And," Rachel went on, looking into the glass half-full of bourbon, "I would try not to talk about Julie and love-making because I knew how he would get. But if I didn't tell him, he would threaten me. 'You are entirely under my control,' he would say. 'I can do anything to you I want to, so you better do what I say.' And he was right. I was. I had to do what he said. It was kind of a paradigm of the situation of men and women—the situation which I have so long opposed and tried to change."

"Not only Lawrence but his mother," Susan said.

"Yes. She, too. The matriarch. Trying to prevent the world from changing and making what she had always been seem unimportant, or even worse, silly."

"I wonder how conscious they were of that," I said.

Susan shrugged.

Rachel said, "Not conscious, I think. But subconscious. It was a kind of dramatization of the way they wanted the world to be."

"Who took your clothes?" Susan said.

"The mother. I assume she wanted to demean me. She had Lawrence and the other one that worked for them strip me when they took me to that room."

"I wonder if that might have been for Lawrence, too," Susan said.

Rachel drank some more bourbon. She held some in her mouth while she looked at Susan. "Perhaps. I hadn't thought of that. But perhaps she had some sense that he was not sexually ordinary. Maybe she thought the chance for a nice uncomplicated rape would help him along." She finished the bourbon. I poured her some more without asking.

Susan said, "You haven't said anything very much about how you felt about all this. You've told us what happened. But maybe it would be good to get some feelings out."

"I don't know," Rachel said. "I have learned to keep my feelings under very strong control. Maybe not so different from himself here." She nodded at me. "I have had to, doing what I do. I'll write about the feelings. I write better than I speak. I do know that being a captive is a humiliating, a debasing experience. To be in someone else's hands. To be without control of yourself is terribly destructive of personality and terribly frightening and terribly . . . I don't know quite what I want to say. Terribly . . ."

"It ruins your self-respect," Susan said.

"Yes," Rachel said. "You feel worthless. That's just right. You feel contemptible, almost as if you deserve the mistreatment. As if you're somehow at fault for being where you are."

"And the sexual mistreatment merely intensifies the feeling, I should think."

Rachel nodded. I opened another beer and drank most of it. I had little to offer in this conversation. I gestured the beer bottle at Susan. She shook her head.

Rachel turned and looked at me. She sipped some bourbon and held the glass toward me. "And you," she said. For the first time there was just a faint blurring in her speech. "There are things I need to say to you. And they are not easy to say. While I lay back in your bathtub and tried to soak some of the filthiness of this all away, I thought about what I should say to you and how." She looked at Susan. "You are invited," Rachel said to Susan, "to help me with this. Maybe you have some sense of where my problems lie."

Susan smiled. "I'll pitch in as needed," she said. "I suspect you won't need me."

"There are a lot of things that don't need to be said," I said.

"But these things do," Rachel said. "I always knew that if someone found me, it would be you. Somehow whenever I fantasized being rescued, it was never the police, it was always you."

"I had more reason," I said.

"Yes, or you would see yourself as having more reason, because you would perceive yourself as responsible for me."

I didn't say anything. The beer was gone. I got up and got another bottle and opened it and came back and sat down.

"And you did it the way I expected you would. You bashed in the door and shot two people and picked me up and took me away. Tarzan of the Apes," she said.

"My brain is small, I have to compensate," I said.

"No. Your brain is not small. If it were, you wouldn't have found me. And having found me, you probably had to do what you did. And it's what you could do. You couldn't remain passive when they wanted to eject me from the insurance company. Because it compromised your sense of maleness. I found that, and I do find that, unfortunate and limiting. But you couldn't let these people kidnap me. That, too, compromised your sense of maleness. So what I disapproved of, and do disapprove of, is responsible in this instance for my safety. Perhaps my life."

She stopped. I didn't say anything. Susan was sitting with her heels caught over the bottom rung of the chair, her knees together, leaning forward, her chin on her left fist, looking at Rachel. Her interest in people was emanant. One could almost feel it.

Rachel drank some more bourbon. "What I am trying to do," she said, "is to thank you. And to say it as genuinely as I can. I do thank you. I will remember as long as I live when you came into the room and got me, and I will always remember when you killed them, and I was glad, and you came and we put our arms around each other. And I will always remember that you cried."

"What'll you charge not to tell?" I said. "Makes a mess of my image."

She went on without pausing. "And I shall in a way always love you for those moments." Her glass was empty. I filled it. "But I am a lesbian and a feminist. You still embody much that I must continue to disparage." She had trouble with *disparage*. "I still disapprove of you."

"Rachel," I said, "how could I respect anyone who didn't disapprove of me?"

She got up from the dinner table and walked softly and carefully around to my side and kissed me, holding my face in her hands. Then she turned and went to my bedroom and went to sleep on my bed.

We just got the table cleared when the cops came.

32

THEY WERE WITH us a long time: the chief of the Belmont force and two other Belmont cops; a man from the Middlesex DA's office; Cronin, the twerp from the Suffolk DA's office; Quirk and Belson.

Cronin wanted to roust Rachel out of bed, and I told him if he did, I would put him in the hospital. He told Quirk to arrest me, and Quirk told him if he couldn't be quiet, he'd have to wait in the car. Cronin's face turned the color of a Christmas poinsettia, and he started to say something, and Quirk looked at him for a minute, and he shut up.

We agreed that I could give them a statement and that they would wait until morning to take a statement from Rachel Wallace. It was late when they left. Cronin gave me a hard look and said he'd remember me. I suggested that his mind wasn't that good. Susan said she was very pleased to have met everyone and hoped they'd have a Merry Christmas. Quirk gave her hand a small squeeze, Belson blew smoke at me, and everyone left.

In the living room Susan and I sat on the couch. The fire was barely alive, a few coals glowing in the gray ash.

"We've spent a lot of time here the last few days," Susan said.

"There are worse places," I said.

"In fact," Susan said, "there aren't too many better."

"We may spend a lot more time here, because she's in our bed."

"The final sacrifice," Susan said.

"We could think of ways to make the best of it," I said.

"You had to kill two people today," Susan said.

"Yeah."

"Bother you?"

"Yeah."

"Want to talk about it?"

"No."

"Sometimes people need to get feelings out," Susan said.

"Perhaps I could express them sexually," I said.

"Well, since it's for therapy," Susan said. "But you'll have to be very quiet. We don't want to wake Rachel up."

"With half a quart of bourbon in her?" I said.

"Well, it would be embarrassing."

"Okay, you'll have to control your tendency to break out with cries of *atta boy* then."

"I'll do my best," she said. "Merry Christmas."

Much later we heard Rachel cry out in her sleep, and I got off the couch and went in and sat on the bed beside her, and she took my hand and held it until nearly dawn.